THE CHERRY VALLEY MIDDLE SCHOOL NEWS

DEAR KNOW-IT-ALL!

★ ★ ★

Digital Disaster!

by RACHEL WISE

Simon Spotlight

New York London Toronto Sydney New Delhi

SIMON SPOTLIGHT
An imprint of Simon & Schuster Children's Publishing Division
1230 Avenue of the Americas, New York, New York 10020
Copyright © 2013 by Simon & Schuster, Inc. All rights reserved, including the right of reproduction in whole or in part in any form.
SIMON SPOTLIGHT and colophon are registered trademarks of Simon & Schuster, Inc.
Text by Veera Hiranandani

For information about special discounts for bulk purchases, please contact Simon & Schuster Special Sales at 1-866-506-1949 or business@simonandschuster.com.
Manufactured in the United States of America 0213 FFG
First Edition 10 9 8 7 6 5 4 3 2 1
ISBN 978-1-4424-7217-4 (pbk)
ISBN 978-1-4424-7218-1 (hc)
ISBN 978-1-4424-7219-8 (eBook)
Library of Congress Control Number 2012954934

Chapter 1

MIDDLE SCHOOL GIRL ATTEMPTS HIGH-WIRE ACT AND SURVIVES!

★ ★ ★

Life can be a real balancing act. My mother always talks about trying to "find balance" in her life. She wants to spend time with me and my older sister, Allie, drive us places, help us with school, and all that. She also needs to do her work and take care of the house, the bills, and whatever else adults have to balance. She certainly has a lot going on, and I know exactly how she feels.

What could a middle school girl have to balance, you ask? Oh, nothing—just friend stuff, family stuff, schoolwork, and my school newspaper responsibilities, which include being an investigative reporter and the top-secret columnist Dear Know-It-All for the *Cherry Valley*

Voice. People write in with their difficult issues, or occasionally their ridiculous issues, like *Dear Know-It-All, how can I stop getting gum stuck in my hair?* Um . . . don't put gum in your hair? I do my best to answer these questions, but nobody can know I write the column. It's not easy keeping a secret like that, especially from my BFF, Hailey Jones.

So I have to balance all that and, of course, my lifelong crush on Michael Lawrence, who is the cutest boy in the universe and who works on the paper with me. Whenever we're on the brink of becoming more than friends, the article we're working on gets in the way. But responsibilities come first, I guess, and I'm really serious about being a journalist when I get older. I'll admit, it's a lot to handle, especially when things get tough at school, tough at the paper, and tough at home all at the same time. This is one of those times—*Middle School Girl Attempts High-Wire Act and Survives!* I hope.

I had been studying for our third-quarter math exams all week and it was my last night of cramming before the test. Yesterday, I had just "put to bed" (as Mr. Trigg, the *Voice* advisor, calls it) my latest story (which means you finish it) and the Dear Know-It-All column. I *also* had a language arts paper due. Allie was studying for a bunch of tests and had papers due and was practically psycho, demanding the house be absolutely quiet so she could concentrate. *Plus*, my mom was swamped with work. She wanted to help us with all our work, but she had plenty of her own. I wanted to wish myself off to the Bahamas.

"Sam." My mom poked her head in my room. "Need any help?"

I looked up from my cross-legged spot on my bed, papers and books lying all around me. Mom had a weak smile on her face and bags under her eyes. I know she meant well, but I also know she just wanted to go to sleep herself.

My mom's really good at math. She's a freelance bookkeeper and really likes her work, but apparently I didn't get the math gene. There are about seventy-five other things I'd rather do than study for math. If I force myself,

I can do okay, but I would rather scrub out the bathroom toilets than study for math. Trust me, I've done both.

"No," I said quickly. I didn't want to add more to her load.

"Sam," she asked again, "are you telling me the truth?"

I smiled sheepishly. "Well, maybe a little with this part." I pointed to the set of equations that were particularly making my eyes spin around. Our school has tried to be more "global" and "organic" about our class subjects, so things are taught in a sort of connected way, like how science, math, and history all overlap, or at least how they can work together. Still, even if we're studying math from a "global perspective" by looking at the way people deal with money in China, for example, math is still math. Writing just comes much more easily to me.

"Hmmm," she said, peering over her glasses. "This is a tough one."

"Well, tomorrow it will be all over," I said, and flopped down on my stomach, pressing my face into my pillow. I lifted my head and looked at Mom. "I really need a break."

"I think we can all use a break." Mom smiled a weary smile. "Let's go to Rosie's for dinner tomorrow night."

"That would be great!" I could already taste the lasagna from our favorite Italian restaurant.

"Good," Mom said. "Now, let's get this finished so we both can get some sleep." As tired as she was, she made sure I knew my math inside and out. I'm lucky to have a mom like that.

The next day I felt ready to take the test and super ready for it to be over. I didn't want to think about math for a while, or at least for a few days! I walked down the hall, not really looking at anyone, making my tired way down the hall to the classroom. I just wanted to be relaxing at Rosie's, sipping on a Coke, the smell of fresh-baked garlic bread wafting all around me.

"Have you gone deaf?" I heard someone saying to me through my garlic bread daydreaming. I turned around. It was Hailey, grinning from ear to ear.

"I've been calling your name for, like, an hour," she said. "Is your mind on who I think it's on?"

"If you guessed garlic bread, you're right."

"Garlic bread? You sure you weren't thinking about you know who?" she asked me, her hands on her hips.

Just as I was about to explain why my mind was on garlic bread, you know who came out of nowhere.

"Hey, Paste," he said, looking as cute as ever in a light blue sweater and jeans.

"You still can't let it go," I responded, referring to his unstoppable need to call me a stupid nickname from . . . how shall we say . . . an "incident" in kindergarten. Like I'm the first kid who ever tried to eat paste.

"Are you ready for the test?" he asked.

"Ready as I'll ever be." I let my backpack slip down my shoulder.

"How about you, Hailey?"

"I just want to pass. I don't set my sights quite as high as you nerds. I've got my athletic prowess to rely on." She flexed her biceps. She actually had pretty impressive biceps, but her calf muscles were really out of control from all the soccer she played. She'd be a great leg model except for the fact that she'd never be caught dead in high heels.

"Well, just speaking for my nerdy self, I don't have any muscles to fall back on, so I better nail it. And, Hailey, you'll do great. When we studied together the other day, you totally knew your stuff."

Hailey's a lot better at math than writing. She also gets to take her tests untimed because she's dyslexic, which means sometimes she sees letters flipped around. She has to work really hard at all her schoolwork, but she has a really logical mind. I love that about her. When I get all dreamy and dramatic, she brings me back to the real world.

"I'm just ready for these tests to be over," Michael said. He was the kind of person who never let anyone see him sweat, but now I could see a little tiredness creeping through his bright blue eyes.

"Yeah. My mom's taking us out tonight," I said, "to celebrate, sort of."

"Oh yeah?" Michael said, perking up. "Where?"

"My favorite place. Rosie's," I said dreamily. Thoughts of bubbling melted cheese started to dance in my head.

"Seriously?"

"Yup."

"That's my favorite, too," he said as the five-minute bell rang. In a second, kids were rushing everywhere. If you were late on a test day, you were immediately marked down a point.

"Gotta go!" he called out, and ran off to his class.

Hailey and I were right near our classrooms.

"Just another thing you lovebirds have in common," Hailey said, and punched me in the arm. "Break a leg."

"Ow."

"You need to work out. Give yourself some options," Hailey said, and winked at me.

"Ha-ha. You break a leg, too." I punched her, but my hand sort of bounced off her arm and then we went to our separate classrooms.

I sat down and got out my perfectly sharpened

pencil. I'm a total pencil geek. I never take a test without at least three needle-sharp pencils in my bag. It's sort of a superstitious thing. Mrs. Birnbaum, my math teacher, handed out the tests and gave us the time on the clock.

"You have exactly forty-five minutes. Please begin," she said, and looked at her watch.

I heard everyone's pencils start to make little scritch-scratch sounds and I hadn't even picked up mine. Suddenly a wave of anxiety washed over me. *Newspaper Nerd Fails Math and Drops Out of Middle School.* Stranger things have happened.

After the first few very tough questions, though, I got into a groove and relaxed. When I finished the last question on my test, ten minutes ahead of time, I put my pencil down and stretched, feeling strangely refreshed. I could actually go home tonight and do absolutely nothing except eat lasagna and go to sleep. It was a difficult test, but I'd worked hard and survived.

"How'd you do?" Hailey asked me when we met at our lockers after.

"I think I did okay. Maybe not an A, but at least a B," I said, hoping I didn't jinx myself.

"Me too." Hailey smiled.

We gave each other a high five. When I got home, my mom was waiting for me in the kitchen with a mug of hot cocoa. "Well?" she said, standing at the counter sipping from a mug.

"Pretty good . . . I think." I sat down, and she squeezed my arm. That's another thing I love about my mom—she doesn't freak out if we don't get straight A's all the time. She just wants us to try and do our best.

"I'm sure you did great."

Then Allie came home, walked into the kitchen, and let her bag drop to the floor.

"Hang it up, or in your room please," Mom said, pointing to the bag.

"I think I'm going to drop out of school," Allie said, and picked up her bag. She looked on the verge of tears.

"What is it, honey?" Mom's eyebrows quickly knitted together in their worried way.

"I got a D on my history paper. And I think I

just failed my chemistry test."

She dropped her bag again on the floor, but this time Mom didn't say anything. Then Allie slumped down on the kitchen stool next to mine. She put her head down over her arms on the counter. Now I was worried.

"Allie," Mom said in a slow, gentle tone, kind of like she was talking to a crazy person, "you've been working so hard. What happened?"

Suddenly Allie lifted her head and smiled. "Psych!"

"Huh?" I said, choking on my hot cocoa a little.

My mom stared wide-eyed at her as Allie thrust out her history paper.

"A minus! And I think I rocked chem. Or at least I didn't fail. Bring on the hot cocoa! And do we have any cookies?"

"Allie, not funny," Mom said.

"You have a bizarre sense of humor," I said.

"Well, you're just bizarre," she zinged back, but she was smiling and nudged my shoulder with hers.

"Cheers," she said, and held up her mug. I couldn't help but clink back.

That night I had possibly the best lasagna of my entire life. The best part, though, was all of us relaxing and having fun together. I felt like it had been a long time since the three of us had done that. And boy did we all need it.

Chapter 2

MYSTERIOUS SCANDAL ROCKS SCHOOL TO THE CORE

★ ★ ★

On Monday morning at school, after a nice weekend of mostly sleeping in and watching my favorite shows I'd DVR'd but hadn't been able to watch for, like, a month, Michael came running up to me while I was trying to unstick the zipper on my black fleece jacket. Even though it was technically spring, it was still pretty cold.

"Hey, Sam, did you hear about what happened?"

I looked up from my zipper immediately. Michael called me Sam only when something was really serious. He was breathless, his face flushed.

"No?" My heart started to beat really fast. I stuffed my hands in my jacket pockets and braced myself for what he was about to tell me.

"Someone stole the math exam."

"Wait a minute, *stole* it? What do you mean?" I asked.

"Well, not stole it exactly. The day before the exam, the math department teachers couldn't get onto the computer system because the password had been changed. They thought an administrator or another teacher had changed it. They were able to retrieve the files, but it took them a day to figure out it was no one on the staff. It probably was a student trying to get the test ahead of time." Michael's hands moved wildly about while he was talking. He seemed upset, but also kind of excited.

"That's pretty serious," I said, but was sort of relieved. I'm just glad it wasn't about anybody getting hurt or something. "How do you even know this?" I asked.

"I saw Mr. Trigg this morning. He told me everything and wants us to do a story on it. We're going to talk about it at our meeting today."

"Wow," I said, trying to get my head around the whole thing. I wondered what it was going to mean for all of us.

I went back to my zipper. I had to be in language arts in less than five minutes and I still had my jacket on. I tugged it down as hard as I could, but no luck.

"Let me help you there, Pasty," Michael said. Before I could respond, he grabbed the zipper and gave it a hard pull. Finally my jacket opened and there Michael was, standing there still holding the zipper. We stared at each other.

"Uh-oh," he said.

I couldn't help but laugh. "Thanks a lot, Lawrence!"

"I guess I don't know my own strength," he joked, but then he lowered his eyes and looked uncomfortable. "I'm really sorry. Can I buy you a new jacket?"

I was speechless. He was too good to be true, this Michael Lawrence. "Uh." I forced myself to say something. "That's really nice to offer, but I'm sure my mom can fix it." I stuck my hand out for the zipper. "At least I don't have to wear my jacket to class, so thanks!"

His smile returned. "No problem. Any time

you need your clothes ruined, you know who to call."

I laughed and he handed me back my zipper. I couldn't wait to tell Hailey about this, and I couldn't help but wonder what he would have done if I'd taken him up on the new jacket offer. Would we have gone shopping together? Maybe I had just made a big mistake turning him down. After I put my broken jacket in my locker, Michael and I walked together to class. His seat was right in front and I was in the middle. We sat down. The room was buzzing. Everyone all around me was already discussing the big news. How had people found out so fast? Mr. Farrell, our teacher, was trying to get the class's attention by turning the lights on and off. It took a while for people to settle down. *Mysterious Scandal Rocks School to the Core.*

I wondered who was stupid enough to do something like this, if that was the case. The truth was, no one knew what had actually happened. But if it was a student, had he done it because he was really afraid he'd do badly on the test, or had he just wanted to cause some major drama? I looked around. It could have been anyone, maybe even someone right in this room! Finally people started to settle down.

Mr. Farrell cleared his throat extra loud. "I know many of you are concerned about the very serious situation with the recent math exams," he said in a stern tone. "There will be an announcement made later today about it," he continued. "In the meantime, ladies and gentlemen, we have to focus on the here and now."

The here and now was going to be a new unit on Edgar Allan Poe. Mr. Farrell started by reading the poem "The Raven." I was anxious to find out about the test, but Mr. Farrell was going full force ahead. There was nothing to do but listen to the poem and wait for the announcement. The dark and mysterious nature of the poem sort of fit the mood.

At lunch Hailey and I got a table together. I could tell she was buzzing with the same energy we were all feeling, sort of upset, sort of excited. Why are bad things exciting sometimes?

"What do you think is going to happen?" she asked, taking a bite of her only lunch item, a big roll with butter.

I had the Mediterranean chicken salad, the organic food option we had in our lunchroom that day. It had olives, tomatoes, and couscous in it. Pretty tasty, but it probably made Hailey think of her mom's superhealthy cooking too much, which was always chock-full of things like veggies and "whole grains." When Hailey isn't at home she eats the most horrible not-nutritious food you can imagine.

"I really don't know," I said, chewing thoughtfully. "They're not even sure about what happened or if anyone actually looked at the test or the answers."

"I heard they're having some special computer people come in to do an investigation," Hailey said, spreading a big wad of butter on her roll. Her mom would be so mad if she ever saw Hailey's lunches, but I've been sworn to secrecy.

"Wow. Why would someone do something like this?"

Hailey shrugged. "Do you think we might have to take the test over?"

My stomach did a flip. In the back of my mind I'll admit I'd had the same thought and quickly pushed it away. Suddenly I wasn't so hungry anymore.

"If we do, I swear I'll make it my mission to find the person who did it and personally give them a piece of my mind. Michael and I are going to do a story on it for the paper," I said.

"So maybe you will actually find out who did it!"

"They better beware." I meant it. It's one thing to make your own mistakes, but to ruin things for everyone else, like me, who worked hard and followed the rules. It made me so mad.

"It's sure livened things up around here," Hailey said, looking around. You could see people huddled around talking, and if I had to bet, I'd guess most people were talking about exactly what we were talking about.

After we left the cafeteria, I was having a hard time concentrating on my earthonomics class. But just before the next class began, the principal's loud booming voice came on the loudspeaker.

"Good afternoon, students of Cherry Valley Middle School. I have an important announcement to make," Mr. Pfeiffer began. You could hear a pin drop. "I'm sure most of you have heard that there has been a security breach in regard to the third-quarter math assessments. We have started an investigation, but at this point the results of the exam are invalid. A new test schedule will be sent home by the end of the week and all seventh-grade students will be retested. Thanks for your understanding during this trying time. Please direct questions to your teachers or to me. Remember, gossip hurts everyone."

The microphone went off and the silence continued. My cheeks felt hot as the news sank in. I'd actually have to take my math test over! The one that I'd studied a whole week for! It was so unfair!

I looked up at Mrs. Birnbaum. She was pacing in the front of the room, her arms crossed, shaking her head. She seemed as upset as I was. But she didn't have to take the test over.

"This brings up a lot of important questions and issues," she said after a moment, addressing the class. "This disrupts everyone's schedules, including the teachers. I do find myself angry. But it's hard to be angry when you don't know who to be angry at."

Sophie Meyers, who sat in the front, was on the math team, and was basically known for being a straight-A student, raised her hand.

"Yes, Sophie," Mrs. Birnbaum said, pointing to her.

"I just can't believe someone could be so selfish. I work really hard to do well. And now I'll have to work even harder because someone else was lazy and dishonest." Sophie's voice shook a little from her strong emotions. I was surprised that someone like Sophie Meyers was so upset. Doing well seemed to come so easily to her. But I guess getting straight A's wasn't easy for anyone. I also realized these were great quotes for the *Voice* article. I got out my notebook and started to write down what Mrs. Birnbaum and Sophie were saying.

"Well, first of all"—Mrs. Birnbaum sat down on the front edge of her desk—"at this point we don't even know if it was a student who hacked into the system. But I understand how you feel, Sophie. The entire math department will have to create a new exam in the next few days. More work for you guys means more work for teachers, too. It's unfair; no way around it."

"If it was a student," Will Hutchins said, and paused for a moment before going on, "maybe the kid was really stressed out. Maybe his or her parents were coming down very hard. This person might have reacted out of fear, not really thinking about how it would affect other people. It just might not be so black and white—the hacker is bad, others are good."

I put my pencil down and looked at Will. He was the kind of kid who never stood out that much. He was quiet in class and really into computers and he was in the IT club. He was actually one of the students helping the paper change over to a new online format. I'd barely even remembered he was in the class until he spoke up. It was a good point, and a brave one to make, since I couldn't help but think that the kind of kid who did this might be just like Will.

"That's a really good point, Will," Mrs. Birnbaum said. "It's important to remember all sides to this issue and not to jump to any judgments until we hear all the facts."

"But even if the kid was stressed out, it doesn't make it okay. We all feel stress," Sophie said, now glaring at Will.

"These are *all* really good points," Mrs. Birnbaum said, "and a lot to think about. But we're going to have to stop here and get some things done today. Remember, if you're feeling overwhelmed, please come to me or any teacher and ask for help. There's a lot of pressure on students these days. Don't be afraid to reach out."

We started a new unit, but my mind was swimming with all these quotes I was collecting even before officially starting the article. This was going to be big.

At the *Voice* meeting, Michael, who is always running late, was actually there before

I was and had saved me a seat.

"I've already got some great quotes for the piece," he whispered in my ear.

"Me too!" I whispered back.

"Nice," Michael said. The room was all abuzz. Mr. Trigg had to clap his hands loudly to get our attention. Everyone finally quieted down.

"Greetings, fellow journos! So we had some big breaking news, folks," Mr. Trigg said. "We want to handle this well. As Churchill once said, 'With great success, comes great responsibility,' and I can think of no better words for this occasion."

Michael looked at me and rolled his eyes. Trigger, as we liked to call him, always started quoting Winston Churchill when he got excited, and nothing made Mr. Trigg more excited than a good scoop. I thought about the quote, though, and it definitely rang true.

"So I think we can count on the Martone/ Lawrence duo to investigate this with their usual gusto."

Michael gave a thumbs-up and I nodded, hoping no one would see the color that rushed to my cheeks hearing our names like that.

"But, Mr. Lawrence and Ms. Martone, please remember the wise words of Churchill. This story is big and will get outside press attention, so I want to make sure you guys are up for the task. We will need accurate, spot-on coverage here, which I know you do well. You'll have to be extracareful to fact-check everything. No hearsay. This may be one of the most important stories you work on this year."

More nodding from me and Michael, and then I started to get a tight feeling in my throat. I'd *thought* I was up for the task, but now Mr. Trigg was scaring me with all his Winston Churchill energy. At least I wasn't in it alone. I wondered if Michael was also feeling, as Mr. Trigg would say, just a "tad" overwhelmed.

"The other item on the docket is that this issue will be our first ever online edition. As you know, the entire office just received upgraded computers, so I thought it was time for us to get with the twenty-first century. We will still have a print run, but the entire paper will also be available online instantly the moment we hit the publish button. Thanks to everyone on the IT team for making this change possible."

People started clapping and cheering, and I looked over at the group of students from the IT club who I assumed had come to the meeting for this moment. My eyes traveled over to Will Hutchins. He sat in the back of the group wearing the hood of his sweatshirt pulled over his head, not smiling. Something was a little odd about him. He saw me looking at him and I quickly looked away.

"So I think you have your work cut out for you, folks," Mr. Trigg said, and tugged on the lucky scarf he always wore to the meetings. *Newspaper Advisor Makes Understatement of the Year.* Just when I thought things were calming down.

Chapter 3

CHEATING VIRUS TAKES OVER MIDDLE SCHOOL

Hey Paste! We need 2 get together and discuss article. Wednesday night my house?

That was the IM blinking on my screen when I finally got home. A wave of excitement washed over me. I know Michael wouldn't have asked me if we didn't have the article to do, but still, it was kind of awesome to be greeted with that kind of message.

Sure, what time? I replied, trying to play it cool.

How about 7?

Good. Will there be cinnamon buns? I asked.

We'll see how good your quotes are . . .

I smiled. Michael made these great cinnamon

buns and sometimes he made them when we were working on a story. My mouth started to water just thinking of them. Then I realized I needed to message Hailey. I hadn't even told her about the broken zipper incident and now my work date with Michael on Wednesday night. Life might have been moving a million miles an hour, but at least it wasn't boring!

But before I did that, I wanted to check out my Dear Know-It-All letter stash for the week. I took them out of my pocket and read the first one. *Dear Know-It-All, I'm always losing stuff: my phone, my homework, my favorite glow-in-the-dark rainbow key chain. How can I keep better track of things?* My favorite glow-in-the-dark rainbow key chain? Was this person serious? Next.

Dear Know-It-All,

I had a friend write one of my book reports for English. I hate my English class, and anyway, I'm going to be a singer in a rock-and-roll band, so I don't think speaking or writing perfect English is going to be important to my life. I have another report coming up and I think I want my friend to help me out again. What do you think?

Rock on,

Rock Star

I swallowed hard and put the letter down on my desk. What was going on here? *Cheating Virus Takes Over Middle School.* First of all, the idea of letting someone else write your words for you was appalling enough, and then to take credit for it! It's one thing to wish you didn't have to write something, but it's quite another to do what Rock Star had done. It was hard to deny that writing skills were important, even for a rock star. What about writing songs? What world was this person living in? I had so much to say to Rock Star that I felt like I could spontaneously combust at any moment.

"Dinner!" my mom called, and my racing head stopped. I took a deep breath and stashed the letters in my secret spot under the bed. I needed to take a step back and think about Rock Star later.

I went into the kitchen and sat down. Mom had made spaghetti and a salad. At that moment, I realized how hungry I was. I heaped up my plate, twirled a big mouthful of spaghetti on my fork, and took a bite.

"So have you started studying for your math test again?" Allie asked in a teasing voice with a smirk on her face.

I looked up at her, my mouth still full of spaghetti.

"What do you mean?" Mom asked before I could say anything.

"Apparently, some crazy computer nerd hacked into the math department's test file and Sam's entire grade has to take their tests over again."

"Oh no. That's terrible!" Mom exclaimed.

"I have a notice about it in my backpack and, anyway, nothing's been proven," I said, glaring at Allie, still making my way through my bite of spaghetti.

"Well, who else would have done it?" Allie

gave her long blond hair a defiant flip from one side to the other and looked at me questioningly.

"It could have been anyone. You can't make assumptions," I said, stabbing a cucumber and waving it around for emphasis. "But the file was definitely hacked into, so that makes the test results invalid." My shoulders slumped as I said the word "invalid."

"I'm sorry, Sam. That must feel really frustrating," Mom said. "You studied so hard."

"Frustrating is one way to describe it." I started to feel the rage build up again. Rock Star popped into my head, not that I thought Rock Star was the hacker, but Rock Star was also in that category— the cheater category. It was hard for me to believe there were people out there who were willing to lie and cheat to get what they wanted no matter who it affected.

"Well," said Allie, "I kind of wish that would happen to my chemistry test. I would have loved another few days to study."

"No you don't. What a ridiculous thing to say!" I said, suddenly raising my voice.

"Allie." Mom held up her hand. "Sam is obviously upset about this, and what happened is really awful on so many levels. It's nothing to take lightly. Please try to be supportive." Then she turned to me. "And, Sam, I know you're upset about it, but there's no reason to yell. Just take a step back. Allie's not who you're mad at."

I leaned back in my chair and took a deep breath. Mom was right. I wasn't mad at Allie, but she could be so annoying sometimes.

"I'm sorry," I said to Allie, kind of meaning it. "It's hard, though. I don't know who I'm supposed to be mad at. The bright side is I'm doing a story for the paper on it."

"With lover boy?"

"Allie," Mom said sharply. "That's enough."

Allie's mouth clamped shut and she crossed her arms. I felt a twinge of satisfaction.

Mom turned back to me. "Well, that will certainly be an interesting subject. Are you going to be able to be objective about it?"

Mom had a good point. Reporters were supposed to be objective, not favoring one side or the other. How could I get to that place when I was so angry about what had happened?

"I hope so," I said, and twirled up another bite of spaghetti.

When I was done with dinner I went into the den and called Hailey. Too much information for an IM. I needed some voice time.

"Hi," she said, sounding out of breath when she answered the phone.

"What were you just doing? Running laps around the house?"

"Practicing handstands. Builds up your core."

"Oh yeah, that's what I was doing, too," I said.

"Really?"

"Uh, no." I have never done a handstand that didn't end in me crashing to the floor and almost breaking my neck. "So Michael asked me on a work date this Wednesday. I don't know if he would call it that, though."

"I think if he asked you to come over and work, it at least qualifies as a work date. See, now that's something positive about the math exam disaster. You have an urgent story that needs attention!"

"True," I said, considering this.

"Who do you think did it?" she asked.

"Someone who doesn't care about anyone else," I blurted out. Then I remembered what my mom said. Be objective, Sam. Be objective. That was going to have to become my new mantra. "No, I don't really mean that."

"Yes, you do!" Hailey said. "I kind of feel that way too, but maybe it was someone who just felt desperate, felt like they had no other choice."

An image of Will Hutchins flashed in my mind. I turned sideways in the big armchair and hung my legs over the arm. "What do you think of Will Hutchins?"

"Why? Did he do it?" Hailey asked in a hushed, excited tone.

"Oh, gosh no," I said. The last thing I wanted to do was spread rumors like that. "I mean, I have no idea. He just had a lot to say about it in my math class and seemed weirdly sympathetic to the hacker."

"He's a little strange," she said. "I'm surprised he had a lot to say. He's in my language arts class and never says a word."

"Yeah, I was surprised myself."

"Well, maybe you should interview him for the paper," Hailey said, her voice sounding suddenly far away and breathless again.

"Another handstand?" I asked her.

"Yeah, have you on speaker," she called out.

"You're insane," I said. Where did she get her energy?

"No, you are," she said, and then I heard a crash and a yelp.

"Hailey?" I asked, panicked.

"I'm okay," a small, faraway voice said.

After Hailey recovered and assured me she hadn't broken anything, I told her about the morning jacket incident and then her mom told her she had to get off the phone and do her homework. I had to do mine, too.

Back in my room, I took another look at Rock Star's letter. This time I sat on my bed in a cross-legged position and took slow breaths in and out the way Allie had showed me from a yoga class she'd taken. *Reporter Turns to Yoga for the Answers.* Why not? I needed all the help I could get. Even though it wasn't my job to be objective as Know-It-All, I thought I should practice, so at least I could be levelheaded about it. I breathed in, and as I let my breath out I whispered, "Be objective." Then I read the letter again. Maybe that's all she or he could see, the rock star dream, and it truly felt like nothing else mattered. But then when I got to the part where it said that Rock Star wanted his or her friend to "help" out again, my blood started to boil. What you really mean, Rock Star, is that you want your friend to "help" you cheat in your language arts class again and not only risk your own standing in school but your friend's as well. Ugh! Maybe I wasn't as good at this objective reporter thing as I thought.

In the morning I got to school early and officially started my piece by doing some man-on-the-street interviews about the math department security breach, as it was officially being called. I had those unofficial quotes from math class the other day, but I'd have to go back and ask Mrs. Birnbaum, Will, and Sophie for permission to use them.

The first two interviews were what I expected.

The seventh-graders I talked to lamented how unfair it was that they had to take a test over just because of someone else's bad decision. I knew I was going to get a lot of quotes along this line. I mean, how could someone not feel that way, right? But I summoned my inner objective reporter. I needed another view, something unexpected, something that would show another side to the story. Then I saw Will Hutchins walking down the hall. He wasn't wearing a hoodie, which made him look a little more accessible. He was looking down at the floor, his hands tightly holding the straps of his backpack. I took a deep breath and went up to him.

"Hi, Will. Can I talk to you for a sec?" I asked, clutching my notebook to my chest.

He looked up at me, then looked behind him as if he wasn't sure I was really talking to him.

"Uh, sure," he said when he realized I was actually talking to him.

"I'm doing a story about the test scandal," I said, and then paused to clear my throat. That wasn't really an objective way of putting it. I started again. "I mean, the security issue with the math department computer files."

He smirked, but didn't say anything.

"I just wondered," I went on, "if you had any other thoughts about it, um, besides what you said in math class."

"Not really," he said back.

"Yes, but—"

"Feel free to quote me." He continued walking past me, down the hallway. I watched his back as he disappeared around the corner. Something was going on with that kid. *Middle School Reporter Discovers Suspect!* I know I was getting carried away, but "objectively" Will's behavior was suspicious, whether he intended it to be or not.

A few minutes later I saw Michael coming down the hall.

"So how's it going?" Michael said, coming up to me, pointing to my notebook. "Got anything good?"

"I don't know if I've earned my cinnamon buns just yet," I said, and sighed, leaning against a locker. Then I lowered my voice, turning to Michael. "Do you know Will Hutchins?"

"Yeah, sort of. What about him?" he asked.

"I don't know. He had a lot to say about the test sca—I mean, security breach—in math class the other day. He was saying that maybe the person who did it was really overwhelmed and didn't realize how much chaos it would cause."

"Really, he said that?" Michael sounded surprised. "Do you think he was talking about himself?"

"I doubt it. I mean, who would be that obvious? But then this morning when I asked him if he wanted to say more, he said he didn't and just walked away."

"I guess this story is just going to get more and more interesting."

"I guess so," I said. *Be objective. Be objective,* I thought over and over as Michael and I walked to class.

I got some pretty good quotes by Wednesday. Michael hadn't said anything about our work date since he'd IM'd me on Monday. Is it possible that he'd forgotten? Should I just come right out and ask him if we were still on? I needed a consult with Hailey ASAP.

Finally lunch rolled around and I walked into the cafeteria slowly, looking around for Hailey before I saw Michael. Then, out of the corner of my eye, I saw the back of Hailey's head talking to someone. I started booking over there until I realized she was talking to, you guessed it, Mr. Michael Lawrence himself, along with some of his friends from the baseball team.

"Hey, Paste," he said when he saw me. "What's up?"

"Hi," Hailey said, a big smile on her face.

"Hi," I said back, feeling a little flustered. "So how are your quotes going?" I blurted out.

"Really, really awesome," Michael said, and smiled. He whipped out his notebook. "Want to sit here and talk about it?"

"Uh, yeah," I said, staring at Hailey so she'd get that I was trying to tell her something. "But Hailey and I just have to, um, go over some stuff for something. Right, Hails?"

Hailey looked at me, confused. "Yeah . . . that stuff," she said, trying to figure out what was going on.

Michael looked at me and then at Hailey. Now he was confused. They both stared at me.

"You okay?" Michael asked, turning his head to one side.

"Yes, I'm fine," I said, gathering myself. "What I mean is, why don't Hailey and I go over . . . that stuff . . . and then come over to your table?"

He just nodded. "Great."

When Michael had turned to grab his backpack off the table, Hailey gave me her "what the heck is going on?" shrug. I gave back my "just ignore me; I'm out of my mind" eye roll.

"You know what. I have to talk to Frank," Michael said. "Maybe I'll catch you after lunch, okay?"

"Okay," I said weakly.

"What in the world was that all about?" she said when Michael finally left.

"I know I was acting like a freak. But now I still don't know if I'm supposed to go over to his house tonight. I wanted to talk to you before I saw him. That obviously didn't work out."

"Well, why didn't you just ask him?"

"I felt funny about it."

"Sammy, I'm still going to be giving you the same advice about Michael when we're seniors in high school."

"You're probably right," I said, and sighed. How do I get myself into these things? "So what should I do now?"

Hailey gave me an exasperated look. "Just ask him!" she said. "Hang out by his locker, look real cute, and say something like 'Hey, Lawrence, are we on tonight?'"

"I don't know," I said. Hailey rolled her eyes. Where was all this shyness coming from? Hailey was right. My crush on Michael was probably going to stay just a crush forever. "But no pushing me into him this time or anything!" A while ago, Hailey had developed the incredibly annoying habit of shoving me into Michael whenever we saw him to try to move things forward between us. Not a good plan.

"Scout's honor," Hailey said, and crossed her fingers.

I hoped she'd stick to it, but now what was I going to do? Track him down and ask him, or not? For some reason I was still thinking not.

Chapter 4

YOUNG JOURNALIST SINKS ARTICLE OUT OF FEAR OF INVITING HERSELF OVER

★ ★ ★

I didn't see Michael for the rest of the day. I came home, did my homework, and barely said a word through dinner. Afterward, I threw myself on my bed. I looked over at my computer. All I had to do was turn it on and message him. Why was it such a big deal? Maybe I had just wanted him to confirm with me because he was the one who invited me. The truth was, though, that we had to meet soon and start figuring out our angle for the article. If it wasn't tonight, then it had to be tomorrow. *Young Journalist Sinks Article Out of Fear of Inviting Herself Over.* I had to get in the "business" frame of mind and not worry about what Michael would think, like, immediately. I did a little Allie-style breathing and turned on my computer. I had to be brave and message him. What if he thought I was blowing him off? As the computer was starting up I heard the phone ring. Allie bounded into my room.

"Don't you ever knock?" I asked her.

She held up the cordless phone she'd been holding behind her back. "It's lover boy," she whispered, and handed me the phone

I glared at her and took the phone. "Hello?" I said, sounding like I had no idea who it was.

"Hi, Sam. It's Michael," he said.

"Hey," I said, playing it all cool.

"I thought you were coming over?" he said now, a worried tone in his voice.

"Oh! I'm sorry. I—" Ugh. I wasn't even sure what to say. "I didn't think you said a time, and then I wasn't sure if we were still on, or if I should call you, and I was going to message you, but . . ."

"Well, can you come over now? We've really got to get started." His worried tone was now turning into an impatient one.

"Yes, of course. I'll be right over!" I said, praying my mom would let me, and hung up the phone.

"Sam, why didn't you tell me this earlier?" Mom was already in her sweatpants, making popcorn for the dance contest show she and Allie watched every Wednesday night. Sometimes I joined them, if I was in the mood to listen to Allie criticize the dancers, who all seemed pretty awesome to me.

I wasn't about to explain to my mom everything that had gone through my head about it. "I forgot, and Michael just called wondering where I was. We really have to work on the article."

She looked at me and sighed. "I understand. I just wasn't planning on heading out. It's hard to keep up with your schedule!" She poured the popcorn into a bowl and grabbed her car keys. "Allie!" she called. "Be back in ten minutes! Just dropping Sam off at Michael's!"

Allie appeared out of nowhere.

"I didn't know you had a hot date," she said. "And that's what you're wearing?"

I looked down. I was wearing jeans and my favorite green T-shirt. I was comfortable, and green looked good with my hair.

"It's my lucky T-shirt," I said, my hands on my hips. "And for your information, I'm not going on a date. It's for the paper."

"Wait one sec," she said, and skidded off in her socks toward her bedroom.

"Allie," Mom called. "We're going."

She appeared again in five seconds flat with a purple sweater, boots, and hanging earrings.

"Just put these on! Trust me."

My mom rolled her eyes, and I was about to tell Allie she was crazy. I just wanted to put the work first and not get wrapped up in my crush. This article was super important, and possibly, as Mr. Trigg had said, the most important one I'd work on all year. Still, I couldn't help myself.

"Okay. Maybe you're right," I said, and started changing right there in the middle of the hall.

"Oh, Sam, you looked fine," Mom said, jingling her keys. "The train is leaving in T-5."

I pulled on my boots and stood up to fluff my hair. "Okay?" I asked Allie.

She gave me a thumbs-up.

"Thanks!" I said, throwing her my T-shirt. Big

sisters might be annoying, but she was ultimately on my side.

"Have fun!" she called after me.

On the way over, I was happy that Allie had given me her mini-makeover. Who was I kidding? A chance to hang out at Michael Lawrence's house on a random evening? Priceless. I should at least put a little effort into it.

Michael answered the door in a T-shirt and jeans, looking a lot better than I had in my T-shirt—or at least I thought so.

"Pick me up at nine?" I called to Mom. She nodded and drove away.

The house smelled good, but it wasn't cinnamon buns this time.

"Mmmm, something smells delicious."

"Oh, it's just banana bread," he said, shrugging, and walked quickly into the kitchen. I followed him.

His mom and dad were there, putting the dinner dishes away.

"Hi, Sam," his mom said. "You look nice."

Michael looked at me again and his dad nodded and smiled at me.

"You do," Michael said.

"Thanks," I said, giving a little wave, feeling the warmth rush to my cheeks. Now I was wondering if I should have stuck with the T-shirt and stayed under the radar.

Mrs. Lawrence wiped her hands on a towel and looked at me again. "Michael tried out a new recipe for you."

"Mom," Michael said, now a little color rising on *his* face. "I just wanted a good snack, so I made one," he said, trying to sound casual.

"Just giving credit where credit's due." She grinned.

Michael was not only a great athlete and a great writer. The guy could actually bake, and to top it off he was a little shy about it. Swoon. I wondered, though, had he really gone to all this trouble for me, or was I just an excuse to bake something?

"Do you want some?" he asked quickly, as he started cutting the loaf on the counter in slices. I nodded vigorously. He put two pieces on plates and poured us glasses of milk.

"Let's go into the dining room," he said, handing me my plate and a glass of milk.

"Okay," I said, and followed him. We put our food down on the table. I still had my backpack on. I took it off and got out my notebook.

"Use place mats!" his mom called after him.

"Okay," he called back. He turned to me and shook his head in an exasperated way. "Let me get those and my notes. Be right back."

While he left, I stared at the piece of banana bread. I knew it was polite to wait for him to come back before I had a bite, but I couldn't help myself. I pinched off a small piece from a corner and popped it into my mouth. It was still warm and moist and completely amazing. I wondered if his parents could see me from the kitchen.

He came bounding into the dining room with place mats in one hand and a notebook in the other. I quickly wiped my mouth with the back of my hand.

"Started already, snacky?" he joked.

"Ha-ha," I answered back. "I couldn't help myself. You can't leave me alone with warm homemade banana bread. You should be a baker when you grow up."

He smiled and sat down and took a big bite himself. "Pretty good. Needs a little more sugar, though. Yeah, I'm thinking I'll be a professional baseball player and a journalist, with a bakery on the side."

"Sounds good to me," I said, now freely scarfing down the rest. "Okay, Mr. Talented. Let's get down to business."

"I wouldn't call mixing up some banana bread batter and throwing it in the oven a talent," he said, ever modest. Another item for the Michael Lawrence great personality checklist.

"I would, since I can't bake to save my life," I said, thinking of a few months ago when Allie and I tried to bake our mother a birthday cake from a mix. It came out as dry as sawdust and as flat as a pancake because we'd used the wrong amount of butter and had forgotten to get eggs. Mom seemed happy anyway. She even ate some. I could sit here all night and just talk to Michael Lawrence. But Mom was coming at nine and we had an article to write. "Okay, let's figure out our approach," I said, trying to get into serious work mode. "I'm seeing a few angles here." I looked over my notebook. "There's the 'this is so unfair' kind of comment. Then there were some people who actually feel some sympathy for the hacker, like maybe it was about pressure."

"And there're also people who don't seem to care that much at all." Michael leaned back in his chair, hands behind his head, which showed off the muscles in his arms.

Stay focused, Sam, I thought. "Um, or some people who feel like they're getting another chance to do better at the test," I said quickly, trying to distract myself.

"Yeah," he said excitedly. "So which group do you put yourself in?"

"Me?" I asked, surprised. I had been spending so much time trying to be objective, I had blocked out, or almost blocked out my anger toward the hacker. "I have to admit I'm in the 'this is so unfair' group."

"Yeah, at first I totally felt that way. But now,

listening to all these other opinions, I find myself wondering about the kid who did it. We are under a lot of pressure and my parents are really understanding about that. But what if they weren't? What if they just wanted me to get straight A's all the time because I needed a full scholarship to college or had to go to an Ivy League college just to get their approval. How would I feel then?"

Michael was definitely better at looking at all the sides than I was. "Yeah, I don't know. I don't think you would do that even if you felt more pressure. I mean, how could the person not think about all the people they might affect? I think it's a really selfish way to handle your problems," I said. Honestly, no matter what Michael said, I couldn't feel any sympathy for someone who would make choices that hurt others.

"I just want to make sure we cover the whole story and show every opinion," he said, and made his worried face where he squished his eyebrows together and got this little crinkle in his forehead. "I think student pressure is an important issue."

"It is, but I don't want to lean so far to the other

side where now we're showing sympathy to the hacker. It's still wrong," I said. "I studied hard for that test and it wasn't fun."

"I mean, I'm angry, too, but it's like I'm two people." He took a swig of milk before he continued. "The me that's mad about having to take the test over and the reporter me who's trying to put together a fair story."

Why was it so hard for me to do that? Maybe I needed to back off a bit. Michael was right. "Yeah, of course. I feel that way too," I said. In theory. *Reporter Fakes Sympathy Toward Hacker to Save Writing Relationship.*

"Good," he said, and leaned back in his chair, seeming relieved. "More banana bread before we start to outline?"

"I thought you'd never ask." I batted my eyes. At least Michael could be a bit more levelheaded than I was sometimes. Maybe that's why we worked so well together. It was certainly never boring. And, I thought, biting into my second piece, it was delicious to be working together, too.

Chapter 5

TWO MIDDLE SCHOOL REPORTERS CRACK THE CASE

★ ★ ★

"How was your date last night?" Hailey asked me first thing the next morning at my locker. She looked the way she always looked in the morning—much more awake than I felt. Her hair was wet and shiny from her shower, and her blue eyes shone brightly at me. I really needed to start exercising more, and then maybe I'd feel a little more like Hailey in the morning.

"It was okay and it wasn't a date," I murmured, and piled up my books in my locker. I surveyed the pile—six textbooks one on top of the other stacked a foot high. Maybe Cherry Valley Middle School students were under more pressure than

I allowed myself to think.

"Just okay?" Hailey said, jumping in between me and my locker to get me to look at her. "Did you have your orange juice this morning?" she asked me, her hands on her hips, head leaning to one side.

"Yeah, why?" I said, still in my own thoughts.

"You seem a bit blah."

"I don't know what I was expecting from last night," I said. "I guess I just hoped it was going to feel more special than just working on the paper. He did make banana bread, though," I said, now putting my language arts anthology and a science textbook in my backpack.

"Well, I have never, ever had a boy make me banana bread," she said, grabbing some of her books and stuffing them into her backpack. "So that's something."

"It was really yummy," I said, and smiled. "And I think he did make it just for me. He knows how grumpy I get without good snacks around."

"Sam!" said an urgent voice behind us. I

looked around. It was Michael, sneaking up on me again. I wondered if he'd heard anything.

"Why are you calling me my actual name?" I asked.

"Where's the fire, Lawrence?" Hailey asked.

"What?" Michael said to Hailey, with a confused look in his eye. He turned back to me and said in a low tone, "Sam, can I talk to you for a sec? In private?"

"Just my stupid attempt at a joke," Hailey said.

"Oh right, fire. That's funny," Michael said, turning to Hailey, mustering a distracted smile. "Sorry, Hailey. It's about the story we're working on."

"Uh, sure," I said, raising my eyebrows at Hailey. She shrugged back and motioned for me to go with him. "Everything okay?" I asked Michael. I couldn't imagine what was making him act so weird.

"Yeah. I . . . just a sec," he said, and grabbed my arm, pulling me away from Hailey and down the hallway around the corner. We stood in a quiet space near the boys' bathroom.

"You're kind of freaking me out, Michael," I said, now getting a little annoyed. "This had better be good." Then again, he'd grabbed my arm, which was still kind of tingling.

"I got a quote from Will Hutchins," he said. "Here. Look." He thrust out a piece of paper. "I didn't want anyone to see it yet."

I looked down at his narrow, almost illegible handwriting. Michael wasn't perfect in every way. He had some of the messiest handwriting I'd ever seen. *Question:* it said. I read out loud what I could make out underneath. *"What do you think about the bath rest security beach?"*

"No, no," Michael said. "Math test security breach!"

"Right, of course. Sorry," I said, looking back down. Boy, I needed some orange juice.

"Oh, let me just read it to you," he said, and grabbed the paper out of my hands. "So I asked Will what he thought about the—"

"Bath rest security beach?" I said, grinning.

"Very funny. This is what he said, though: 'I think in some ways the hacker opened up two important issues. Our school has to think about why some kids might be so stressed out, and it also shouldn't be so easy to hack into the exams on the school server,'" he read to me from the paper.

"It almost sounds like he knows who did it," Michael said. "And seems to put the entire blame on the school."

Whoa. *Two Middle School Reporters Crack the Case.* Were we reading too much into this, or could we actually be on to something? "Should we tell someone?" I said in a hushed tone. "It does sound like he's really close to the issue, like he has something personally invested in it. Could he have been the hacker?" I said, now feeling the excitement and urgency Michael was feeling.

"I do think we should tell someone, but who? I don't want to get the guy in trouble if he's just speaking his mind."

"Let's start with Mr. Trigg and see what he thinks," I said as the class bell rang.

"Good idea. I'll meet you in his office after

school," Michael said to me as we started down the hallway toward our classes. "And keep it quiet. I wouldn't even tell Hailey. Rumors can spread like wildfire."

"Okay. I promise," I said, not quite sure if that would be possible. Technically I had already told Hailey that I thought Will was weird. Uh-oh. But I wouldn't tell her that we had a quote from him. Hailey might feel the same temptation to tell just one other person and so on and so on until the whole school would suddenly start thinking Will Hutchins was the hacker. But was he?

Hailey came bounding down the hallway obviously looking for us.

"Well, if it isn't Clark Kent and Lois Lane. What's the big emergency?" she asked, looking back and forth from me to Michael.

"It's nothing," said Michael. "I've got to go." With that he rushed off to class.

"What's with him? Can you tell me what's going on?" Hailey said.

I really, really wanted to. It was hard enough

keeping my Know-It-All drama from her, and now this. I took in a deep breath and counted in my head as I let it out. *One. Two. Three. Four. Five.* "This is all I can tell you. We got a suspicious quote from someone for the article and we need to talk to Trigger about it."

"From who?" she asked, and leaned toward me. "From Will Hutchins?" she whispered, her eyes aglow with the possibility of scandal.

"That's exactly why I can't tell you, whether it was from him or not. It's too big a deal to start rumors. We could really mess with someone here." As I was saying it, I realized how big a deal this really was. "I hope you can understand, Hails," I said.

Hailey looked down at the floor. I didn't want to hurt her feelings. Then she glanced up.

"I won't tell a soul. Don't you trust me?"

I bit my lip and thought about it. If I told just Hailey, what harm would it do? But then what if she had the same thought about another friend and they thought that about someone else? . . .

"I promised Michael I wouldn't while we were

working on the story. It's not that I don't trust you, but I want Michael to trust me."

"Fine. I get it. I guess Michael and the paper are more important." She walked off in a huff, leaving me standing there, my arms dangling by my sides. Was I putting Michael and the paper first? I wasn't sure. I walked to class alone. Why did Hailey have to be so sensitive about things? Sometimes when stuff with the paper heated up and I had to work with Michael a lot, she got upset about something. Maybe she was jealous about the time I spent with Michael, but it was always the worst time for me to have to deal with friend stuff when I was dealing with *Voice* stuff.

At the end of the day, Michael and I met outside Mr. Trigg's office and knocked on the door.

"Come in," he said. We shuffled into the office. His feet were up on his desk and he was enjoying one of his classic cups of tea. "Well, Ms. Martone and Mr. Lawrence! What brings you here on this glorious day?"

It was actually kind of cold and rainy.

"Glorious" would not be the word I'd use.

"Reminds me of London weather," he said, as if reading my mind. "I love those gray days that make you want to curl up with some biscuits and tea and a good newspaper." He took his legs off the table and sat up. "I'm glad you're here. I wanted to ask you how the new online system is going. I have a feeling it's going to make things a lot easier."

"I'm excited to use it, but we haven't finished the article yet," I said. "It's shaping up nicely, though."

"Um, yeah, except that," Michael said, getting right into it, "we got a quote today that seemed . . ." He looked at me, suddenly at a loss for words.

"Troubling," I said.

"I see. What kind of troubling?"

Michael handed him his notes. Mr. Trigg put on his reading glasses and squinted at the paper.

He stumbled through Michael's handwriting. "What do you think about the bath . . . rest . . . Sorry, chap. I can't quite make this out."

"It's okay. I'll read it," Michael said, sighing,

and read the quote out loud.

"Well, that's a juicy bit," Mr. Trigg said, smiling. "Good work!"

Good work? Had Trigger gone off the deep end? I cleared my throat and spoke. "Yeah, but he sounds like he's almost trying to defend himself or might know the person who did it," I said a little louder than I should have.

"Ms. Martone," Mr. Trigg said. "It's up to you to cover the story from all angles and present it as objectively as possible. Don't go jumping to conclusions. There's a team of people investigating the breach. That's not your job."

"But what if he did it? Is it okay that we do nothing?"

"He just gave an opinion. He didn't confess anything," Mr. Trigg said. "I appreciate you telling me, though. I just don't want to start a witch hunt. Is that all?" He got up to press the button of his electric teapot.

"I guess so," Michael said.

"Well, it looks like your article is on its way to being brilliant. Keep going."

Michael and I walked out of his office and into the hallway. We both didn't say anything for a moment.

"That was weird," Michael finally said.

"I know. Not what I expected. I thought Mr. Trigg would definitely want to alert the authorities."

"Maybe he knows something we don't." Michael rubbed his chin in a particularly cute way.

"What do you mean?"

"Maybe he knows who might have done it, and he knows there's nothing to worry about where Will's concerned."

Huh. I never thought of that. "That would make sense then. But how would he know something that we don't?"

"Who knows what happens in faculty meetings? All the teachers probably know things that we don't about this and everything else."

I nodded. I just couldn't shake some sense of responsibility I had, probably because we were the only students actually investigating this story.

"Well, got to go to practice," Michael said. "I'll catch you later!"

I walked home in the rain. Luckily, I had taken Allie's super-cool plaid green umbrella, which she would probably be looking for right about now. Whoops. Still, I felt soggy and tired when I came home. Allie wasn't home yet. I said hi to my mom, who was huddled in her office, made myself a peanut butter and jelly sandwich, poured a big glass of milk, and sat in my desk chair. I took a bite of my sandwich and twirled around a bit. I wasn't sure if I should call Hailey. I kind of wanted to wait until she was less mad.

I lingered over a few of my go-to news Web sites. I knew I was trying to avoid the stack of homework piled up on my desk. I had a vocabulary test, some math homework, and a book report due tomorrow. If I felt overwhelmed, though, which I sometimes did, I asked my mom for help. She always knew what to say to keep me calm, organized, and moving forward. I always felt proud when I finished something I thought I couldn't. If I cheated on a test or had someone else write my book report for me, I would never feel proud, just bad and guilty. How did the hacker and Rock Star feel right now? Maybe they just didn't care about feeling that way. I decided to take another crack at the Know-It-All letter.

Dear Rock Star,

I understand that you may think a rock star doesn't need to know how to write well, but how do you know you'll actually be a successful rock star? Anyone with half a brain in their head needs to know how to write. Plus, you'll be writing songs. To write great songs you need to write well. Also, I'm wondering if you realize that you put your friend at a huge risk when you asked him or her to essentially cheat with you. It's one thing to make your own stupid decisions, but it's even worse to involve other people. Why don't you try writing the paper yourself for once? If you do badly, following your argument, it won't matter since you're planning to be a "rock star" and all. Then you can be honest about your choices and leave your poor friend out of it.

I sat back and read what I wrote. It was clear, direct, and to the point, and exactly what Rock Star needed to hear, at least in my opinion. And I was proud that I hadn't written "YOU'RE AN IDIOT!!!" anywhere, which was what I really wanted to say. I would show it to Mr. Trigg the next day and cross one more thing off my list.

Chapter 6

GIRL SAVES FRIENDSHIP WITH A SLEEPOVER

I didn't see Hailey until lunch the next day. When I walked into the cafeteria, she and Michael were sitting with Jenna and Kristen, Frank, and a couple of other people. I approached them with my tray. Hailey looked at me and then kept right on talking to Michael. She might as well have punched me in the stomach. I sat down quietly at the other end of the table.

"Hey, Paste!" Michael said when he saw me. "Why are you sitting all the way over there? I saved a seat for you." He patted the empty chair next to him.

My heart sped up a little. Banana bread and saved seats. Is this how all guys treated their "friends"? I wasn't sure if I felt comfortable sitting right near Hailey, but how could I pass up an offer like that? I managed a little smile and moved over. I picked up my veggie pizza and took a bite. Yum. It was one of our most delicious options from the organic table. I don't know how the chef made whole wheat crust and broccoli taste so good, but she did. I chewed quietly for a moment.

"Hi," I finally said to Hailey, and waved my hand at her. I was tired of this ridiculous silent treatment. I hadn't done anything wrong. I was just trying to keep my promises.

"Hey," she said, and turned to talk to Jenna. The blood rushed to my face. She couldn't be serious.

"Did you hear that a special teacher/parent meeting is planned for next Tuesday to discuss the retest?" Michael asked.

I snapped out of my Hailey thoughts and looked up. "Really? When did this happen?"

"My mom told me last night," Michael said. "It was e-mailed to all the seventh-grade parents yesterday. I was surprised too."

"Oh" was all I managed to say. I wondered why my mom hadn't told me. I thought of her last night, doing work in her office. She was probably so busy she forgot. Normally, I understood when Mom had a lot of work, but I couldn't help feeling a little angry and embarrassed that as a reporter for this story, I was the last to know. Maybe she needed to do a little rebalancing.

"So, we definitely need to be at that meeting," he said, seeming kind of surprised by my lack of words.

"Yeah, definitely." I was trying to focus on Michael and the meeting, but I had too many thoughts swirling around my head at once. I saw Hailey look at me out of the corner of her eye.

"Hailey," I said a little louder than I meant to, "can we talk for a minute?" Suddenly everyone at the table was looking at me.

"Uh, sure," she said, surprised.

"Over there." I motioned to an empty table. She followed me and sat down. I sat across from her.

"Are you really this mad at me?" I asked,

"because I don't get it, Hailey."

Hailey swung her legs back and forth and looked down at the table before answering.

"I just feel like every time you work on a big story for the paper with Michael, I become second fiddle. I mean, when was the last time we had a sleepover or just hung out all weekend and went to the movies? I know I'm busy with stuff too, but we should always be able to make time to have fun."

I took in a deep breath. Hailey was right in some ways. I did get a little obsessed with the paper sometimes and it had been a long time since we had just hung out all weekend.

"Why couldn't you just tell me that? I wanted to keep my promise to Michael just like I would keep a promise to you," I said. "I don't know why you had to get so mad about it and give me the silent treatment."

Hailey's face changed from angry to a little sad. She looked down at her lap. "It just made me a little jealous that you had a secret with Michael and not me. I know. That's pretty stupid."

It's true that I didn't really have to share Hailey with anyone else. We had other friends, but no one that made me feel "second fiddle," as Hailey had said.

"I have an idea," I burst out. "Next Friday we should be done with the article, and now that the paper is online, it's going to be even quicker to post it. Let's plan a sleepover/movie night, okay?"

Hailey smiled her big sparkly smile. "Okay!" *Girl Saves Friendship with a Sleepover.* Now I could cross off two more things on my list: 1. Dear Know-It-All letter, check. 2. Making up with my bestie, check.

"Hails," I said, grabbing her shoulders, looking her right in the eye. "You're irreplaceable, okay? Not second fiddle at all. And you know all my secrets that really matter."

She nodded again and smiled.

"Want to go back to the other table?" I asked. She said yes, so we walked back over and sat down. Everyone was suddenly quiet with blank expressions on their faces, as if they hadn't been discussing mine and Hailey's drama at all.

"Everything okay?" Michael asked, breaking the silence, a worried look on his face. It was sweet that he seemed to care so much about me and Hailey.

I gave him a double thumbs-up. Hailey nodded.

"So," I said, "why do you think they called this parents' meeting? And who called it, the administration? The PTA?"

"A group of students wrote a letter of protest about taking the test over, signed not only by them, but by their parents. It's becoming a bigger issue than anyone thought. So I think the school administration called it."

"Well, it's good for the article at least," I said. "I'm sure we'll get a lot of great quotes at the meeting."

"Yeah, and maybe when it's all said and done, we won't have to take the stupid math test over," Michael said. I nodded emphatically.

"I kind of don't mind," Hailey said. "It'll be good to have another chance at . . ." She stopped midsentence as my mouth dropped open. "Don't look at me like that, Sam!" she exclaimed. "If I could take every test two times I probably would. It's easier once I've already been through it."

"I'm sorry. I was just surprised." I felt bad that I'd reacted so strongly. I was so in my own head, I'd never considered Hailey, of all people, would have a different opinion than I did. When I thought about it for a second, I understood why Hailey felt that way. Tests had always been hard for her. "Do you mind if we quote you for the article? We want a good balance of opinions," I said, whipping out my notebook.

Hailey's shoulders straightened up and she beamed at me. "Sure!"

After school Hailey had soccer practice and Michael had baseball. It was a perfect time for me to show Trigger my response to Rock Star before I officially e-mailed it. I marched down to his office, my response clutched tightly in my hand. I glanced around to make sure no one was nearby. I knocked the secret knock—two quick knocks and then a third. Mr. Trigg and I had made it up so he would always know it was just me with a Know-It-All question or a draft I wanted him to look at. I heard Mr. Trigg chuckle upon hearing our secret knock.

"Enter at your own risk, Ms. Martone," he called out.

I walked in and he was squinting at his computer, his glasses slipped down on his nose.

"Is that the new paper template?" I asked after seeing the screen. It had the *Cherry Valley Voice* at the top and looked just like the printed version, except it was blank, just filled with empty boxes where the articles were supposed to go.

"Yes. Isn't it splendid?" he asked, but he didn't sound like he thought it was so splendid.

"Yeah, it looks very cool." I sat down next to him, gazing at the screen. A ripple of excitement ran through me. The paper was going to look amazing and all we had to do was drop our text into the boxes. "It's going to make things so much easier."

"That's the idea, except I can't figure out how to get any text in here," he said, pointing to one of the empty boxes. "They showed me several times. I guess it's hard to teach an old dog new tricks."

"Whoa! Slow down, Ms. Martone. I see this has tapped into something for you," Mr. Trigg said. "Maybe you need a little distance. Put it down for a while; then give it another whirl."

"I just work hard to do well and be honest. Aren't you upset by it?" I asked. He was a teacher, for crying out loud.

"Of course. But since Dear Know-It-All is anonymous, there's nothing I can do about it. These kinds of decisions catch up with you. If Rock Star isn't caught now, he or she will have to suffer the consequences at some point. That I'm sure of. But your job is to offer some sound, levelheaded advice, and I know you can do that."

"I hope so," I said, folding up the letter and putting it in my pocket. But I was worried that it might not be possible for me to be "friendly" to Rock Star.

Chapter 7

WORKAHOLIC MIDDLE SCHOOLER TURNS TO NAIL POLISH FOR COMFORT

At home after dinner I went straight to my room to write another version of the letter. I tore the first draft up into little pieces, wrapped it in a tissue, and threw it out in the bathroom garbage can. I couldn't be too careful. I've caught Allie before snooping around in my room. At times I've really thought she was on to me, but then again, Allie just likes snooping, so it's hard to tell.

I opened up my password-protected file and started again.

Dear Rock Star,

I understand that you may think writing isn't a useful skill because of your interests, but didn't you need to know something about writing to write this letter? Do you think this is the last letter you'll ever have to write? And what if you don't become a rock star? Then where will you be?

I stopped typing and read it back. Ugh. I knew it sounded too opinionated. Delete. Start over.

Dear Rock Star,

I took a deep breath and stretched my arms up in the air before continuing.

It's one thing to cheat. It's another thing to ask your friend to cheat for you. I'm surprised she or he agreed.

I read it back. Ahhhhh! This just wasn't working. What I really wanted to say was *Dear Rock Star, what are you thinking????* Everything else felt like a lie. I needed a break or at least another perspective. I heard the thumping of Allie's music in her room, and usually the louder the music was, the worse a mood she was in. I decided to take my chances and knocked on her door. She didn't answer. I knocked harder.

"What?" she yelled back. Hmmm, maybe it wasn't the best time to bug her.

"It's me," I called over the music.

"Come in!" she yelled.

I opened the door. She was sitting on her bed painting her toenails a sparkly blue color. She had one foot propped up on top of a newspaper. I sat down.

"Careful. You're shaking the bed," she said, holding up her nail polish brush.

"Sorry." I gingerly lay down on my stomach, my chin on my hands, and watched her paint her pinkie toe. She was really good at doing her own nails. They always looked professionally done. Whenever I tried, I went through a bag of cotton balls and lots of nail polish remover, correcting the mistakes. Then the smell made me sick and I wondered why I even bothered. Luckily, nothing made Allie happier than doing people's nails.

"Can you do mine?" I asked, cheerfully wiggling my fingers at her.

"Is that why you came in here? What's up,

really?" she said, focused intently on her toes.

"Can't I just come and say hi to my sister?" I asked in a dramatic tone.

"Hi. Now what's going on?" She looked up. "You seem kind of mopey and confused about something. Boy trouble?"

Allie knew me so well. I usually came into her room for three things: friend advice, boy advice, or fashion advice. This reason, though, didn't quite fit into any of those categories, but I couldn't actually tell her why I was asking. "Not boy trouble. Actually I was just working on my article about the test scandal. Wanted your opinion." It was kind of true.

"Yeah, did they catch the guy?"

An image of Will Hutchins popped into my head. "How do you know it's a guy?" I asked.

"I don't, but I just can't imagine a girl doing that," she said.

"You never know," I said. "What if you knew the person who did it? Or if you knew that they had asked a friend to help them actually, *and* they asked you if they should do it all over again.

What would you tell them?" I asked, hoping I wouldn't give anything away.

"Whoa," Allie said, and sat straight up and lowered her voice. "Holy cow! You know who did it?"

"Oh no! Definitely not." Darn. I should have known that was what my question would sound like. Now I was going to get myself in another mess.

"Are you telling me the truth? Swear on our mother's life?" She gave me one of her super-intense stares.

"Chill out, Allie. Of course I don't know who it is. I wouldn't keep that to myself. I'm just asking because I think I know someone who might know who did it, but I'm not even sure about that. It's all very hypothetical," I said, but I was starting to confuse myself. I was trying to re-create the situation with Rock Star and apply it to the hacker incident since that was public knowledge. Now I wasn't sure if I was asking about Rock Star or Will Hutchins.

"Well," Allie said, then paused to blow on her

toes. "I'd tell them that they were a royal idiot. Nice friend, too," she said, and blinked at me. "I mean seriously, who would be so stupid?"

I laughed. I should have known that the only person who was going to be more opinionated about this issue than me would be Allie.

"What's so funny?" she asked.

"Nothing. I just like your answer. Have you ever cheated on anything?" I asked her. Even though Allie was opinionated, I had always wondered this about her. She was a pretty good student, but hated math and science and was usually more into her friends and dance classes than her schoolwork. Could she ever have been tempted?

She was quiet for a moment. "Why do you want to know?" she asked, very interested in her toenails again. She had finished one foot and was starting on the next.

"No particular reason. I've just been thinking about the subject a lot since all this happened." I tried to sound casual, but I could tell Allie had something on her mind.

She stopped painting and put the brush back

in its bottle, screwing the cap on slowly. Then she looked at me and sighed. "I probably shouldn't tell you this, but I cheated once, in eighth grade. It was algebra. I wrote some stuff on my hand for the test and my teacher caught me. I got an automatic F for the test. It was awful. He called Mom and watched me like a hawk for the rest of the year. It was so embarrassing, and the most ridiculous part about it was I would have gotten a much better grade if I had never cheated. Lesson learned!" She lowered her eyes at me. "Don't ever do it."

"I wasn't planning to," I said. "Why didn't I know about this?"

"Mom promised to keep it between me and her. I think she didn't want to put any bad ideas in your head. As if," she said, and started blowing on her feet again.

I sat up, shocked that I'd never known Allie had actually done something like that. "What's that supposed to mean?"

"Well, you're so into school, you know? It seems so easy for you. I just got really overwhelmed and felt like I had to do really well all the time. Now I can handle things better and ask for help when I need it."

I stared at Allie. She thought school was easy for me? Ha! I felt like I never stopped working. In fact, sometimes I felt like I was way too stressed for someone in middle school. I thought of Hailey saying how we hadn't had a sleepover in a while. It's true that doing well in school and with the paper was important to me, but had it become too important?

"School is anything but easy to me," I said. "I just get really wrapped up in whatever I'm doing and don't do anything else. But I'm always stressed. That's my problem."

Allie finished her toes and started clearing up the newspaper. "I guess things are never exactly what you think they are."

I nodded. That was true. "Okay, so I'm going to try to have more fun. Can you paint my nails?" *Workaholic Middle Schooler Turns to Nail Polish for Comfort.*

"I think a little Aqua Fantasy is in order," she

said, taking out a bottle of a bright greenish blue and shaking it. "You won't be able to not have a good time with these nails!" Maybe she'd be right.

After my nails dried, I wrote another draft of the Know-It-All letter and e-mailed it to Mr. Trigg. He'd had a secret e-mail account set up just for me. Sometimes I liked to e-mail him and sometimes I went by, like I had the other day, just to get an immediate reaction. As I was writing, I kept staring down at my nails for inspiration and pretended I felt as friendly and fancy-free as my nails looked. It had to work this time.

Chapter 8

WRITING PARTNERS FLIRT THROUGH ENTIRE MEETING. MISS EVERYTHING.

Finally Tuesday evening came around. Michael and I sat in the auditorium waiting for the meeting about the test scandal to begin. We had both gotten there early and sat in the front row in order to hear and see everything. I'd wondered if we would go together, but Michael had to meet me there after his baseball game and dinner with his team. My mother drove me, but she sat with some of the other mothers she knew and let me have my own space with Michael. I didn't even have to ask her. She's just a cool mom like that. Hailey was there as well, but she sat with her mom. She told me to work hard so we'd have extra fun this weekend. I looked over at Michael, who was tapping his pencil on his notebook. I couldn't help admiring his strong hands for a moment. The old me would think that I was distracting myself from my work, but the Aqua-Fantasy-nail-polished me thought it was just fine. I might be working, but it didn't mean I couldn't crush on him a little bit.

We still hadn't heard anything definitive about who might have done it, but I knew the article wasn't about cracking the case; it was about reporting the events that had happened and the effects it was having on our community. I was also anxious to get the meeting over with, finish the article, and have the same amount of fun my nails seemed to be having. Lots of people had been coming up to me asking me what kind the polish was so they could try it too. I smiled thinking that Allie was a pretty cool trendsetter. And I have to admit, just talking about nail polish made me feel like the kind of girl who wasn't always bogged down by her responsibilities and has, well, fun. Why couldn't I be both?

"Cool color, Paste," Michael said, pointing to my nails with his pencil. Wow. Now even a boy was noticing. This stuff was magic. "Maybe I should call you Nailsy," he said, and nudged me with his shoulder.

"Now, that's just weird." I gave him my best flirty smile and nudged him back. I was wearing a green blousy shirt that looked great with my nails and my lucky little silver hoops. Once again, just because I was here for an article didn't mean I shouldn't look my best.

"Yeah, guess you're right," Michael said. "Pasty fits you better."

"You're hilarious," I responded, still grinning. This meeting was turning out to be much more fun than I had thought. ***Writing Partners Flirt Through Entire Meeting. Miss Everything.*** I had better get into pay-attention mode or else.

I looked around. The place was packed and more people were piling in. Then Mr. Pfeiffer came up to the podium. He tapped on the mike for a few seconds and cleared his throat. A hush fell over the room. Michael and I had our pencils at the ready, all set to take note-taking.

"Good evening, parents and students of Cherry Valley Middle School. An unfortunate incident has led us here, but hopefully we can come together as a community to strengthen our communication. As you know, the administration and the faculty have decided to reschedule the third-quarter math assessments for next Tuesday," he said. Some students booed in the back. He paused for a second and continued a little louder. "Many parents and students are upset and confused about why the current test results can't be used. We're here to explain this to you. This is an open forum where voices are meant to be heard, but remember one thing." Mr. Pfeiffer took off his glasses. He cleaned them on the corner of his jacket and then started speaking again. "Look. We all want the same thing—the best educational environment for our children. Let's not attack one another, folks." With that, he stepped away from the podium and sat down in one of the seats reserved for administrators.

Then the head of the math department—my math teacher, Mrs. Birnbaum—took the mike. She explained exactly what had happened: The day before the test, no one could get into the math department files and all the test information, the exams, and the answers were deleted. They did have backup files, but after several IT professionals looked at the system, it was determined that it had been hacked into by an unknown user, the password changed, and the files printed before they were deleted. The person who did this was still unknown, but the investigation had some promising leads.

"At this time we have no way of knowing whose test results are the product of obtaining the answers ahead of time. The answers were printed out and may have been distributed. We know the retest is inconvenient, but in order to ensure that everyone has the same opportunities, we think this is the best option," she said in a firm tone. Then she opened the meeting up for questions.

Michael's father stood up. I looked at Michael, but he had his eyes glued to his dad.

"My son is an excellent student," he said. I glanced at Michael and saw the color rise to his cheeks. I didn't want to embarrass him further, so I kept my eyes straight ahead. Mr. Lawrence went on. "He's also very committed to several sports and his work on the school paper. I understand that though the results aren't valid, there are other options. We can omit all test grades from the record. I just don't see why my son, who I'm certain has not played a part in this and studied very hard for that test, has to add more to his busy schedule because of someone else's mistakes. Has this option been seriously considered?"

I turned around and scanned the audience. I saw many people nodding in agreement. A few parents and students started cheering. Then all the way in the back, I saw Will Hutchins standing against the wall, his gray hoodie pulled over his head. His face looked serious, with barely any expression at all.

Suddenly lots of parents and students stood up, one after the other taking each side. Then everyone began talking over one another and

Mr. Pfeiffer had to step in.

"We've heard everyone's opinions," Mr. Pfeiffer said, "and Mrs. Birnbaum explained why we have made the decision we made. The reason we can't throw out the grades is that unfortunately many more students will be negatively affected when their grades for the year are averaged. The final tests are weighted to equal more of your child's grade. In order to be as fair as possible, as Mrs. Birnbaum said, we need to retest to ensure that no one had prior access to any answers. We hope the students who studied hard for the exam the first time are well prepared already and need only a refresher study session for this test. While we appreciate all your opinions, this is what we've decided, and we need to now move on. Thanks for your time."

I would have spoken, but so many people had already said many times over what I felt. There was nothing left for me to say. I nudged Michael again. I wanted him to take a look at Will standing so ominously in the back, but when I turned around again, he was gone.

"What?" Michael asked.

"Uh, nothing," I said. I needed to talk to that kid again.

"I think we got some great stuff as far as students and parents are concerned. Let's get some more teacher opinions while we're here," Michael said. "Then we'll really have all we need."

I nodded, and we both went over to interview the teachers. They were excited to talk to us and seemed anxious to allow their voices to be heard, since the parents and students were really the dominating voices at the meeting. Many teachers reiterated what Mr. Pfeiffer had said. Then we went up to Mr. Evans, a math teacher and the head of the IT club.

"Mr. Evans," I said in my best authoritative reporter voice. "What's your opinion on all this? You must have a specific viewpoint since you've been helping with the investigation."

He looked at us and rubbed his beard for a second. "I guess I do," he said, "but my opinion is pretty much in line with what many of the faculty believe. You simply can't steal the answers to something and think that's the solution to your problem. It may seem like a quick solution. But you're actually starting to stack a row of dominoes against yourself— you didn't study for this test, but you did well. Then your stolen test score qualifies you for an advanced placement class next semester. You had difficulty doing the work in a regular class, and now you're in AP! You fall way behind and are anxious and miserable all the time. Your self-esteem plummets because you think you're stupid. You're not stupid, but you were lazy and made a stupid decision and now may be paying for it for a long time to come."

"Wow," said Michael. "Well put. Thanks for your time."

"Glad to be of service," he said, then smiled and walked away.

"This is awesome. We have an amazing story here. Too bad they don't hand out Pulitzer Prizes for school newspaper articles," Michael said. "You're a great writing partner, Nailsy." He held up his hand for a high five.

"Thanks," I said, smacking his hand. Now

it was my turn to blush. "I think we should meet tomorrow and get all of this down into one coherent piece. Want to come over after school?"

After the words came tumbling out of my mouth, I realized I had just invited Michael Lawrence over without thinking/stressing about it for days, getting advice from Hailey, getting advice from Allie, and then stressing about it some more.

"Sure, and then after we post this, we can celebrate at Spring Fling!" Michael said excitedly.

Right! Spring Fling, where our whole class gets to go to an amusement park for the entire day. No work, no paper, just pure fun. I had totally forgotten about it because I was so stressed out about the story and about Dear Know-It-All. And it was the most fun day of the year. I was really out of balance.

"I almost forgot, with all this going on," I said, sweeping my hand over the auditorium full of concerned and somewhat frustrated parents, students, and teachers. Maybe Will Hutchins had a point—there was a lesson to be learned here.

"So we'll write the rest tomorrow and put it online Monday or Tuesday, and it will be ready for the world to see on Wednesday!"

"Do you think we need more time than that?" Michael asked.

"We have a lot of it in place already. It's really just combining what we both wrote and uploading it to the paper template, which seems a lot easier than it was before. We can actually see the layout and tweak it right before we publish it. Mr. Trigg showed me, or actually I showed him," I said.

"If you say so," Michael said.

"Heelooo, superreporters. Get some good stuff?" Hailey asked as she walked up to us. She had borrowed the Aqua Fantasy, and her turquoise nail fabulousness flashed at me. The color looked even better on her with her tan skin.

"Heelooo!" I said, feeling a little giddy from all the energy in the room. I realized I had been talking very loudly in order to be heard over the sea of voices. "What did you think of the meeting?" I asked Hailey.

"Well, I thought maybe the verdict would

change. I know a lot of people were hoping it would. But still the test is happening," Hailey said.

"Yeah. I think the meeting was just a chance for the teachers to explain why they made the decision they did. I have to admit it makes sense to me." I wondered how Michael felt since his dad was obviously upset about the retest.

"Well, at first I agreed with my dad, but now I get that a lot of people rely on the test to raise their average since the test makes up almost half our grade. It has to be fair. But the teachers said they didn't know how many people had the answers. I don't know anyone or even heard of anyone who got the test answers, so I'm not sure it was as widespread as they think. Whoever did this was pretty private about it," Michael said.

I'll say. But who wouldn't be? I wondered what would happen to the person if they actually found out who did it. Would they be expelled? I scanned the floor to try and find Will again, but no such luck. He had left.

I went home anxious to write up all the notes I

had, so I didn't forget how I wanted to use all the quotes I had gotten. I logged on to my computer and saw that I had an e-mail from Mr. Trigg. I opened it, biting my lip, hoping for the best.

Ms. Martone, better, but could still be friendlier. Still a lot of judgment in the tone of the letter. Sorry. Third time's the charm!

Arghhh! How many times did I have to write this letter? What if I just decided to give up? ***Paper Missing Popular Column. Readers Revolt.*** I couldn't let Rock Star win, though. I decided to put my notes aside and give it another crack. I took some calming breaths, wrote it fast without thinking about it too much, and hit the send button before I read it over a thousand times. Then I worked a bit on the article. But after the meeting and writing another Dear Know-It-All draft, I was ready for sleep.

Chapter 9

NEWSPAPER ADVISOR OFFERS UP TEA AND BAD NEWS

★ ★ ★

"Ms. Martone?" Mr. Trigg came up to me in the hallway after my Spanish class. "Could I talk to you for just a sec?"

"Uh, sure," I said, a little startled. Mr. Trigg never came up to me in the hallway. Sometimes I wondered if he ever left his office.

"Great. Follow me." I followed him, which wasn't easy to do since Trigger walks faster than any teacher I know. When we got to his office I was actually out of breath. He closed the door. I wondered if he was going to tell me he knew who the hacker was. I held my breath.

"Tea?" he said as he turned on his electric pot. I wanted to scream, "NO TEA, JUST GET TO

THE POINT!" Instead I murmured a polite, "No, thank you."

"I read your letter," he began.

Oh, I thought. This is just about the darn Know-It-All letter.

"I think you might want to pick another question," he went on. "This topic just seems too personal for you. I'm also worried you're spending too much time on the letter and not enough time on the article."

I let out my breath and sat down. This was not what I wanted to hear. *Newspaper Advisor Offers Up Tea and Bad News.* In fact, he might as well have punched me in the stomach. Had I lost touch with reality? Why couldn't I write this letter?

"I don't know why it works me up so much," I said in a high, whiny tone, even though I didn't mean to be. "I just work so hard at everything I do and people like Rock Star make me mad."

"I understand. But it's not your job to save someone or teach them a lesson. Rock Star isn't everyone at the school. Most people are honest and try their best. Rock Star just might not be sure how to do that. I'm not saying it's okay, but maybe you know someone who hasn't always been honest but is still a good person. Remember, we all make mistakes. Try to think of that person when you write the letter. Put yourself in their shoes just a little bit. Or pick a different letter."

I thought about it for a second. Allie! Allie had cheated once. She'd learned her lesson and now is probably a better student for it.

"Okay. I think I can do that."

"Good. And remember, the article you're working on is a big one. It needs your focus."

I nodded, thanked Mr. Trigg, and hurried out of his office and off to class.

After school I walked in the door and called out to my mother, "Mom, are you here?" I hadn't told her Michael was coming over today. I hoped she wouldn't be upset. But as long as she didn't have to drive me anywhere, she usually was okay with my last-minute plans.

"Yes, in my office," Mom called. I dropped my backpack in the hallway and went into her office, a little room near her bedroom. She sat in her chair, surrounded by papers, her computer, a calculator, pens, pencils, a highlighter, and a little jar of Wite-Out.

"Got a little work, Mom?" I said, smiling. My work was nothing compared to what was going on in this office.

"Do I ever." Mom rubbed her eyes. "I like my work, but sometimes there's too much of a good thing."

"Sorry, Mom. I know how you feel. I have to finish this newspaper article on the test scandal. Is it okay if Michael comes over and we work on it?"

Mom's face perked up. "Of course," she said in a knowing way. "I wouldn't say no to that!"

"Mom, don't get all weird about it. We just have to finish the article. It's not a date or anything," I said, but in my heart I knew that any time I spent with Michael had date possibilities. I was definitely excited to finish the article, but he was also my friend. I needed a break from thinking about all these serious issues and some more downtime. From the looks of it, so did Mom. That one night at Rosie's hadn't quite cut it.

"I'm not getting weird. I'm too tired to be weird," Mom said, and glanced around her desk.

"Don't forget to breathe," I said. "In through the nose and out through the mouth."

Mom took a deep breath. "Ahhhh, thanks. That does feel relaxing."

I went into my room and looked through my closet. I picked out a cool white T-shirt with a sequined design of a butterfly on it and my favorite jeans. Then I put on a little pink lip gloss and brushed my hair. There. I looked fresh and pretty, but not like I actually spent time getting dressed for the occasion.

I went into the kitchen to see what I could offer Michael. I don't think I could quite equal homemade banana bread, but I could make him my famous microwave popcorn.

I decided to start the popcorn before he came since I was feeling a little snacky, one of Michael's many ridiculous nicknames for me. If I felt hungry, I wasn't going to be any fun. I popped a big bag and was just pouring it into a bowl, lots of steam rising up into my face, when there was a knock on the door.

"Coming," I yelled, and padded over in my bare feet. Allie had also given me an Aqua Fantasy pedicure, so anytime I had the chance to bare my shiny toes, I took it.

"Hi," I said, greeting Michael at the door.

"Hey," he said. "What smells good?"

"Not cinnamon buns or banana bread. So don't get too excited. Just my famous microwave popcorn. I've been cooking all day." I dramatically swept my hand over my forehead. He looked like he had just showered. His hair was still wet and he had that clean soapy/freshly laundered smell. *Crush Smells Way Better Than Popcorn.*

"A snack perfect for a snacky girl," he said. I couldn't help but laugh.

We went into the kitchen and sat at the counter, a big bowl of popcorn between us, and got down to work. We showed each other what we had and started combining and shaping the story.

"So do you think the main point of this piece

is ultimately the huge effect one kid's mistake can have on a lot of people?" I said after a while. Then I took a piece of popcorn, threw it up in the air, and tried to catch it in my mouth. It bounced off my nose and onto the floor.

"Let me show you how it's done," Michael said. He threw one up in the air and opened his mouth. Instead it bounced off his chin.

I couldn't help but giggle. "How on earth did you do that? Show me your secret!" I asked, faking an amazed supergirly voice.

"Ha-ha," he said, and tried again. This time it made it into his mouth. "Score!"

Then I tried and scored as well. We both did it several more times, with more popcorn landing on the floor than in our mouths.

"Okay, back to the question," Michael said, as he helped me pick up the popcorn. "I think so. Also it's about why having the retest was actually important even though many students felt it was unfair. Sometimes what might be good for the whole community is not always what the individual wants."

"I think we covered both sides of both sides. Does that make sense?"

"Perfect sense!" Michael said, and tossed up another piece of popcorn, this time nailing it.

It was nice that we were so in sync about the story. It wasn't always the case when we worked on a piece, but I had been through enough inner drama with the subject matter and was glad that Michael and I ultimately didn't have any major drama while writing it.

"I don't mind typing all this up and e-mailing you what we wrote here so we both have it. Let's upload it tomorrow in the template and we can tweak it online over the next few days. We don't go 'live' until Tuesday."

"Are you sure you don't mind doing that?" he asked.

"No problem," I said. "I'm an expert typist." I flexed my biceps. I didn't mind the extra typing. It actually relaxed me.

"Thanks. Sounds like a good plan, because the day after the launch happens to be the day of the class trip," Michael said. "And I want to be able to enjoy it without worrying about the issue."

"Once again, I like how you think, Mikey," I said.

"Always a pleasure to snack and write with you," Michael said as he held out his hand for a handshake and gave me his award-winning grin. My heart did a little flip as I shook his strong hand.

The next day we put the story up and were able to cut and edit it right in the *Voice* layout. It was much easier than I'd thought it would be, and since we didn't have to get the story in days early and could work right up until pub day, I finally found myself with a little time on my hands. Michael seemed more relaxed about it too. We had only a few spots we wanted to tighten up and that certainly could wait until next week.

I saw Hailey walking down the hall in front of me when I left the *Voice* office and Michael had already left for a late game he had. "Hails!" I called behind her. She had just gotten done with soccer practice and was ready to go home. "So glad I caught you. It's Friday! Movie tonight? Or a sleepover?"

"Both!" she said, and linked arms with me. We walked straight out of school into a day of freedom. On the way out, I saw Will Hutchins holding his backpack tight on his shoulders.

"Hailey, hold on a sec," I said. The girl may leave reporting for a bit, but the reporter never leaves the girl.

She sighed at me and rolled her eyes. "You're obsessed," she hissed at me.

"A little," I said. "Don't worry. I promise it will be short."

I walked ahead of her to catch up with him. "Hey, Will. Do you have a minute?" I called to him as sweetly as I could. He peered at me out of his hood.

"Yeah, I guess," he murmured. "Are you gonna take notes?"

"What do you mean?"

"I mean do you want another quote from me for the paper?" he asked.

Maybe I was obsessed. *School Reporter Comes Dangerously Close to Stalking Student.* Not really, but after this I promised myself I would back off. "No. The article's pretty much done," I said, trying to sound mellow. It was true, sort of. We certainly could add anything we wanted up until Tuesday.

"No, I'm just interested in your point of view since you're a student and . . ."

"And what?"

Good question. What was I going to tell him? *You're a computer expert and have acted suspicious during this whole incident and I want to see if you did it?*

I stood up tall and gathered myself for a second. "And you're a computer expert," I said slowly. "*And* you seem to have some strong opinions on the subject. I noticed you were at the parent/teacher meeting. What did you think of the outcome?" I asked, hoping I wouldn't chase him away.

"I thought"—he paused and took off his hood—"I thought that things are messed up."

"What do you mean?"

"I mean what I just said. It's too bad for everyone—the hacker, the students, the teachers, the parents. It's just messed up."

"So you do think a kid at this school was the hacker?" I asked, slipping into investigative reporter mode.

He just looked at me. "I gotta go," he said in a low tone and hurried away.

Hailey walked up to me. "He's strange."

"He certainly acts like he's hiding something," I said, shaking my head. "But I don't think I'm ever going to find out what it is."

"Maybe not," Hailey said. "But it's not your job. Right now your job is to have fun with me."

"Yes, ma'am," I replied, and we linked arms and sang "Follow the Yellow Brick Road" while we skipped home like lunatics. *The Wizard of Oz* had been one of our favorites in elementary school. Hailey and I have probably seen it together twenty times.

Hailey came to my house and a little later her mom dropped off Hailey's stuff. Allie was at a friend's house, so we didn't have to worry about her yelling at us to turn the music down or being nosy in general. First we checked out Buddybook.

I refuse to actually be a member since I'm afraid I'll get nothing else done if I am, but I keep track of things through Hailey so I'm not completely in the dark. We checked out Michael's page and sifted through some cute baseball pics that some of the team members tagged him in. There was one of him pitching that I kept going back to. He looked so intense and serious. I loved how Michael really put his all in everything he did.

"Hey," I said. "Do you know if Will Hutchins on Buddybook?"

"Uh-oh. Here we go again," she grumbled, but looked him up anyway.

He was. There were lots of pictures of him and his dog and a few of him skateboarding. He actually posted a lot, mostly song lyrics and inspirational sayings. He had a lot of "buddies," which surprised me, and he didn't keep his posts private, which meant you could see them even if you weren't his buddy. They were all public. He seemed like such a loner at school. This was another time things weren't exactly as they appeared. His most recent post, which he made yesterday, really caught my attention, though.

Getting close was all it said. A bunch of people, mostly kids in the IT club, gave a "thumbs-up" to his post, but nobody made any comments.

"Huh," Hailey said. "I wonder what that means."

"See? Now you're getting why I'm obsessed," I said.

"Well, I'll keep tabs on his posts for you," she said. "But now let's get ready for the movies!"

We tried on a thousand outfits, blasted our music, made up some really awful dance moves, and acted just like two girls who didn't have a care in the world.

Chapter 10

MISSING REPORTER FINALLY FOUND HAVING GOOD TIME!

Hailey slept over Friday night and then I went over to her house on Saturday. We spent the day at the mall picking out lip gloss, an awesome new shade of nail polish called Watermelon Slushy, and flip-flops in anticipation of the warmer weather. On Sunday it was so nice outside, after her soccer game Hailey called and asked if I wanted to go on a ride along the bike trail. I was thrilled at the thought of doing something outdoors.

"Sure!" I replied. I couldn't remember the last time I just "played" all weekend long. It felt really good.

"Don't you have a deadline for the paper?" Mom said when I told her I was going on a bike ride. I could tell she was surprised that I suddenly had some free time.

"It's online now, so I have a couple extra days," I said. "We're basically finished."

"If you say so," said Mom, but I could tell she was a little concerned, probably because she was used to me stressing out all the time about the paper. "Your bike helmet's in the garage."

I wasn't lying. We were basically finished with the article, but I still had to get going on another draft of the Know-It-All letter and e-mail it to Mr. Trigg on Sunday night. Still, I definitely had time for a little fun.

Sunday night arrived and I had to come back to earth. The first thing I did was check my e-mail. I hadn't looked at it all weekend, a first for me, at least since I got my own e-mail account. Michael had sent me a message on Saturday and then another one this afternoon.

Are you sure we'll have enough time on Monday to put in the changes we want? Maybe we should meet Sunday afternoon?

And then the next one said,

Where are you, Sam? Did you get my e-mail?? I guess we'll have to take our chances with the article. . . .

I felt bad that I hadn't gotten back to him, but I didn't regret taking my little staycation with Hailey. ***Missing Reporter Finally Found Having Good Time!***

I decided to message him:

Sorry, Mikey. I was just having too much fun this weekend and my e-mail got away from me. Don't worry. The article will be fine.

After a minute, he replied. **I thought you left the country!!!**

Nope, just my computer ☺ I typed back to him. I smiled, wondering if he'd missed me. I stretched out my arms and fanned out my fingers. Okay, now it was focus time. My head did feel a little clearer after taking a break. I thought about Rock Star and remembered what Mr. Trigg had said. I needed to pretend that Rock Star was eighth-grader Allie, overwhelmed with her work and not sure what to do.

Dear Rock Star,

It sounds like writing papers is not your favorite thing. I get that. I really do. There are plenty of times I'm not excited about doing a paper or studying for a test, and I have definitely been overwhelmed by schoolwork. I think a lot is expected of students at our school. Still, what if your friend gets in trouble on your behalf? Or what if she or he makes you look like a better student than you are and then even more is expected of you? The pressure will only increase and the cheating will catch up with you. It always does. Maybe you can get help with your next paper from a tutor, or your parents, or even a friend (who helps you do your work, not does it for you). You don't have to be in it alone. I wish you luck on your road to being a rock star. Good writing skills may or may not play into it, but a clear conscience can only help you be the best at whatever you want to do.

When I finished the last word, I jumped up and threw my hands in the air. "Yes!" I yelled out. I knew I had struck the right note this time.

"What's up with you?" Allie said, suddenly

standing in my room. She leaned in a bit in order to get a better look at my computer screen.

I froze. I had the presence of mind to quickly close out my Know-It-All document before I whipped around.

"What did you just close out of?" Allie asked suspiciously, waving a finger at the computer, not missing a trick.

"Nothing," I said, still gathering my thoughts. "I didn't close out of anything."

"Liar, liar, pants on fire," Allie said, taunting me. "Writing a secret letter to your boyfriend?"

I crossed my arms over my chest. "Seriously, why don't you ever knock?" Not only had Allie ruined my moment of victory; now I was being forced to lie when I just wrote about clearing your conscience.

"Ah-ha! So it is a letter to your boyfriend." She turned and walked out of the room.

"I don't have a boyfriend," I yelled after her. Then I stopped. I needed to let her believe whatever she was going to believe. Better that than her insisting she look at my computer. And it wasn't a total lie. I'd just IM'd Michael, who wasn't my boyfriend, and an IM isn't exactly a letter. But that's my story and I'm sticking with it! I quickly got back on my computer and sent my DKIA letter to Mr. Trigg and then closed out the file immediately. *Nosy Sister Almost Discovers Secret Identity.* Maybe I should be a CIA agent instead of a journalist when I grow up!

At school the next day when I was walking with Hailey, I saw Mr. Trigg in the hallway. He smiled and gave me a thumbs-up. "Nice work on that piece," he said, obviously trying to be ambiguous about it, and then hurried off in his usual speed-walking way before I even got a chance to respond.

"What is he talking about?" Hailey asked.

Oh brother! Here we go again. "I just sent him a part of the test scandal article I was having trouble on," I said without blinking an eye. It was a little scary how good I was getting at this.

"Oh cool," she said not thinking much of it. "I'm so psyched for Spring Fling!" she said.

"Me too, but I'm not psyched for the math test tomorrow." My stomach did a little flip thinking about everything that was going to happen in the next three days. We were going to finish up the newspaper this afternoon, and the dreaded math retest was scheduled for tomorrow. Then we were rewarded with Spring Fling on Wednesday. I should have made a spreadsheet to keep track of it all.

"Well, technically we've already studied for it. It's just reviewing stuff," she said nonchalantly.

I was surprised Hailey was being so relaxed about school. Maybe taking tests a second time really did work for her.

"I just hope I don't do worse the second time around. But I guess I'll never know if I do," I said. The math department had decided not to let us see our grades because some of them could have been invalid and also so people wouldn't be upset if they did do worse the second time.

"The chances of that are pretty low," Hailey said. "You'll be much more familiar with the concepts now, even if the questions are different."

I laughed because it sounded like something Mom would say. "I hope you're right," I said, picking up the pace. The five-minute bell rang and I didn't want to be late for math class today of all days when we'd review for the test.

"And anyway," Hailey said brightly, "before you know it, we'll be screaming on a roller coaster and stuffing our faces with cotton candy."

I was starting to catch her enthusiasm. "Maybe I'll even get to ride the Ferris wheel with you know who," I said dreamily. The Ferris wheel was the most romantic ride I could think of.

"Yeah. And if you get scared at the top, you can grab on to his arm. Better yet, he could grab on to yours!" She was laughing now. "Oh, Sam, my love," she said in a deep voice, between laughs. "Protect me from this frightening Ferris wheel!"

I doubled over and started cracking up so hard I couldn't speak. Hailey makes me laugh harder than anyone on earth. In my opinion, this is a superimportant quality for any bestie.

"Oh no," I said, suddenly straightening up. "We're going to be late!" With that we took off to our separate math classes.

After school I headed to the *Voice* office as soon as I could. I had a few changes I wanted to make to the article and I was sure Michael did, too. Now it was time to get serious and finish our article.

"Well, if it isn't Ms. Leisure," Michael said, coming in right after me. Nobody else was there yet.

"Hilarious. Can't I take a little break?" I asked, putting my stuff over at one of the computers and pulling out a chair. I sat down and pulled up the *Voice* template.

"I'm just kidding with you, Paste," he said, his eyes twinkling. "I'm just used to you bugging me about the story. It was a little spooky the other way around." Michael put his backpack down and pulled a chair over to mine. When he sat down, he was so close, we bumped knees. It felt like an electric current ran through me when his knee touched mine. I stared at it.

"Oh sorry," he said, sounding a little nervous, probably because my eyes were fixed on his knee.

"It's okay," I said, and the image of Michael grabbing my arm on the Ferris wheel just kind of popped in my head. A smile started to spread over my face.

"What's so funny?" he asked.

Like I could even explain. "Nothing. Just excited to put the finishing touches on the story." We took turns adding a couple of things, fiddling with this sentence and that and making sure both of our sections flowed together. Then we read it over for the millionth time.

"Nice work, Sam," Michael said when he finished.

"Couldn't have done it without you," I said, smiling. When Michael called me Sam, I knew he meant it.

After a little bit, the rest of the *Voice* staff started to come in and poke around at their stories. Then Mr. Trigg came in and gave everything a last look before he officially previewed the entire paper.

"Okay, guys, we want it perfect," he said, standing in the middle of the room. "Just because we can launch the paper in the blink of an eye, instead of waiting two days for it to be printed and delivered, doesn't mean we can be any less professional about it. Once it's out there, it's out there. We can't have any trigger fingers."

Just as he finished speaking, an ominous crack

of thunder shook the room as a rainstorm started rolling in. Everybody jumped a little bit at the sound.

"Okay, so let's get ready to preview this thing and see how it looks! I will hit publish at six a.m. sharp tomorrow morning, so we've got to put this to bed today. I don't want people e-mailing me changes at midnight." He clicked the preview button. A murmur of admiration ran through the room as we saw the paper on the screen the way everyone at school would see it. It looked fantastic.

"A smashing success," Mr. Trigg said. "Superb work everyone!" Another blast of thunder shook the room. The lights flickered for a second and then we heard a pop. Suddenly we were standing in darkness. There were a few shrieks, giggles, and screams. At first I didn't understand what happened. One moment we were all cheering the paper; the next we were jostling each other in the dark. A warm hand touched my arm.

"Don't worry, Pasty," Michael whispered in my ear. "Everything will be just fine."

Now I wanted to scream. Wait until Hailey got a load of this—me standing with Michael Lawrence in the dark while he whispered in my ear—even better than being at the top of the Ferris wheel.

"Stay calm, everyone," Mr. Trigg said. "I'll call the front office if—"

But the lights flickering once more interrupted him. Then they went back on and stayed on. Everyone clapped and cheered.

"Okay," Mr. Trigg said. "Now, where were we?" The computers had shut off in the power outage. He turned on the one we were all looking at again.

"Here we are," he said, opening the file for the *Voice* layout again. The masthead came up, but nothing else did. All the text boxes were blank.

"Did I click on the wrong file?" Mr. Trigg asked, bewildered,

"Here. Let me see," Susannah, the editor in chief, said. She closed it down and clicked on a few things. The template came up, but with no text again. "Ummm," she said in a flat tone. "It looks like everything's gone."

Gone? How could that be? Things didn't just disappear like that, or did they?

Mr. Trigg sighed. "An unfortunate accident,

but one obviously beyond our control," he said. "I'm sorry. We'll have to stay here just a bit longer than planned. Okay, everyone, let's retrieve our backups and load them in again."

A tingle of fear rippled through my body. Michael and I looked at each other. *Backup?* I mouthed to him. He shrugged. Gulp.

Jeff, the photographer, seemed unfazed. "I still have all the photos I took in my camera," he said. "I'll just download them again for the stories. No biggie."

A silence blanketed the room. Nobody said anything. I heard someone swallow. I could have heard a fly cough it was so quiet.

Mr. Trigg cleared his throat. He looked a little pale. "*Please* tell me you were paying attention at the start of the semester when I reminded you to always back up your work. *Please* tell me we are *not* going to have to re-create the entire issue from scratch!"

The layout editor and the section editors admitted that they didn't have backups.

"Well, the reporters have backups, right? At least we can load the stories up again. We'll have to do another layout edit, but it won't take us that long. Let's start with the front news section. Ms. Martone, Mr. Lawrence?"

I tried to speak, but my voice seemed caught in the back of my throat.

Finally I managed to speak a few tiny, faraway words. "I have very extensive handwritten notes in my notebook. . . ."

Now Mr. Trigg's face started turning red, very red. One by one he questioned the entire staff. No one—not a single soul—had backed up their work, except for Susannah, but she had written only a couple of short "filler" articles to fill space.

"I—I assumed all my writers backed up their own work," she stammered.

Mr. Trigg started to pace back and forth and rubbed his chin. He took off his scarf, then put it on again. It looked like he might have a nervous breakdown. "Folks, this issue must launch tomorrow. Mr. Pfeiffer is holding a luncheon with members of the school board of directors, and the highlight of the lunch is supposed to be to present our first online edition. So let's think, people.

Winston Churchill wouldn't have let this stop him." Again, silence. Michael nudged me in the arm. "What about what you typed up and e-mailed me?" he whispered.

"I have it," I whispered back. "But we made a lot of changes online. I don't have those."

"Okay," said Michael, now loudly facing everyone. "Let's not panic. We all e-mailed our latest stories, right?" Everyone nodded, some vigorously, some not so vigorously. "So let's load those in and update as much as we can and then we'll all edit online. There are four computers in here. We'll just split up into teams. If we each take a few stories, we should be able to get through this."

I was impressed. Michael was an assertive guy, but I had never seen him take charge like this before. He seemed calm, steady, and I certainly wasn't the only one who felt relieved someone was taking charge. Mr. Trigg's face turned back to its normal color. Susannah relaxed and she, with Michael's help, started getting everyone into groups. The layout team began to re-create the headlines and download each story. The keyboards were clicking and the paper started to come back to life.

"Now, I feel silly having to say this after everything that's happened, but please back—"

"We *will* back up our work after each story is uploaded, Mr. Trigg," Susannah said breathlessly. "And forever after!"

We worked for a few hours; then Mr. Trigg ordered us pizza. Everyone took a break and chowed down. Mr. Trigg came over to Michael with a huge smile of relief on his face and patted him on the back.

"A brilliant Churchill moment back there, Mr. Lawrence. Thank you."

Michael shook it off. "Just wanted to help in whatever way I could," he said, and I could see a little red spreading over his cheeks. I was so proud of him and only more head over heels with the boy. Yikes.

As the hours went by, I tried to ignore the fact that when this was done, I had to go back home and study again for the math test. It was going to be a long night, but hopefully it would all be worth it.

After the reporters had all copyedited their

stories, Mr. Trigg added the Dear Know-It-All column and did another preview. No thunder and lightning could stop us now. We were backed up several times over.

Then the staff crowded around and read the Know-It-All letter. I held my breath, at the same time pretending to be as interested in what it said as everyone else.

"Wow," Jeff said. "What a moron!"

I stopped breathing for a second. Did he mean me or Rock Star? As if he'd read my thoughts, he continued. "I mean the person who wrote in, not Know-It-All."

"Yeah," said Susannah. "Great response."

My heart swelled on hearing that much-needed praise. Only Mr. Trigg knew what I had been through to get it right. I bit my lip to keep from smiling. Someone gave my shoulder a little squeeze. At first I thought it might be Michael. I froze and did not dare turn around. Did he know? But then I saw Mr. Trigg walk away from behind me. Okay, my cover wasn't blown. Onward and upward, as Mr. Trigg liked to say.

Chapter 11

THE SAM TRAIN FINALLY RUNS OUT OF STEAM

★ ★ ★

When Mom drove me home that night it was almost nine. I walked straight into my room and collapsed on my bed. My head was spinning. Everything had been such a whirlwind with the *Voice* and now I had to buckle down and study! I was officially overwhelmed. I didn't have any temptation to cheat, of course, but I sure was tempted not to study and just hope I remembered enough from the last time. Mom and Allie were in the den watching a singing contest show, and the faint sound of someone belting out Adele's "Rolling in the Deep" trickled into my room. I so wished I could just collapse on the couch and watch it with them and forget about everything for a little while. ***The Sam Train Finally Runs Out of Steam.***

There was a soft knock on my door. I knew it was Mom. Allie barely ever knocked, and if she did, it was more like a pound.

"Hi, sweetie," Mom said after I called for her to come in. "Are you okay?"

"Not really." I was lying flat on my back, staring at the ceiling. There were a few thin wavy cracks on it that looked like a demented smiley face.

"You must be pretty wiped out." Mom sat down on the edge of my bed.

"That's putting it mildly. I just don't think I can study for this test again. People who cheat ruin everything," I said in a low, pouty voice.

"Oh, honey." Mom laughed a little. "Maybe so, but you can do this."

"How do you know?" I sat up, facing her. "What if I can't, and then I do badly on the test when I probably did pretty well on the first test? It's all so unfair!" I flung myself back down, crossing my arms tightly over my chest and let out a groan.

"Listen to me." Mom was very serious and looked me dead in the eye. "If you can re-create an entire newspaper in three hours, you can certainly take another hour or two and review your notes. You already know the material. The Sam I know doesn't give up this easily."

"Yeah," I said. "But I just want to go to sleep." I turned on my side and curled my knees into my chest.

"Have you ever submitted a newspaper article without revising it?"

"No," I murmured.

"Well, this is kind of like that—a revision. Think of it as a great opportunity. You rarely get a chance to revise actual events in life. Now's your chance!"

I sat up again and looked at her. Maybe she was right. I had a feeling I hadn't done quite as well as I could have the first time around. It was time to look at the half-full aspect of all this. I could get an even better grade out of it.

"Okay," I said. "You win."

"A bowl of popcorn and some iced tea to help you through?"

"That would be awesome. Mom," I called after she got up and was walking out of my room.

"Yeah?" she turned and asked.

"You're a good mom," I said. Somehow, with all she had to balance, she was always there for me. She was really kind of amazing.

She smiled. "You make it easy."

First thing the next morning I checked the new *Voice* site. As promised, Mr. Trigg had posted it at six a.m. and there were already tons of comments listed. I loved being able to have a sense of what people thought about the paper before going to school. I could prepare myself a little more easily. There were lots of comments about the test scandal and, as expected, many different opinions were shared. But that's what we wanted, a well-rounded but thought-provoking article. Maybe the generation before us wasn't sure, but ultimately I liked this digital world. I was running late, though, and didn't have time to read any of the comments on Dear Know-It-All.

When I got to school, Hailey was waiting for me at my locker. "You're famous!" she shrieked at me. "Your article is the talk of the town."

"Thanks, Hails. I'm glad it actually exists. I haven't even told you what we went through to get it published on time!" Then I gave her the whole rundown, bit by bit, saving Michael whispering to me in the dark for the very last.

"Wow. Your life is so much more exciting than mine right now," she said a little wistfully.

"Well, if it means anything to you, after today, I'd like it to be a little less exciting."

"But tomorrow's Spring Fling, and that has many possibilities for more excitement," she said.

"Okay, after tomorrow." I smiled. She grabbed my arm and started pretending she was Michael again, saving me on the Ferris wheel.

"What's so funny?" Michael said. This time I wasn't even surprised. All we had to do was mention one word about him and there he was.

"Nothing," Hailey and I said in unison, both holding in our giggles.

"Just us being weirdos as usual!" I announced.

I certainly didn't want Michael to think we were teasing him.

Michael glanced at me and then at Hailey. "Well, I can't disagree with that. Listen. I think they might have found the hacker."

Our mouths dropped open. "What?" we said in unison again. Sometimes it was like we were one person.

"I heard something from Frank about a notice being sent home. He heard a teacher talking about it near the main office. Still don't know if it's true, though." Michael looked at me. I wondered if he was thinking what I was thinking.

"Now the day's going to go so slowly. I wish I didn't know that!" I cried.

"But did you see all the comments posted about our article already?" he said, his face lighting up. "You're a rock star!" He gave me that secret I-can-read-your-mind look again. I stood still, a little in shock with all the information coming at me. Was he talking about the Dear Know-It-All letter? I decided to ignore it.

"You mean you're both rock stars! But not like

that dope who wrote in the letter to Know-It-All," Hailey said. "Maybe Rock Star was the hacker!"

"All I know is that I'm glad I'm not that kind of rock star. Hopefully, after the hacker gets revealed it will stop anyone who's thinking of cheating right in their tracks."

"Yeah," said Hailey. "The stupidity of some people astounds me."

"But I liked Know-It-All's response. Rather than just trying to make Rock Star feel like an idiot, which is probably what I would have done, she gave some good, well-thought-out advice," Michael said.

She? Did he know? "Okay!" I yelled, and both Hailey and Michael turned to me, startled. "Um, got to go take that wonderful math test again!" Michael always said stuff that made me think he was on to me.

"Right," Hailey said sort of slowly, trying to figure out why I was freaking out.

"Good luck!" Michael called after us.

We hurried to our classes and only because she was probably feeling nervous for her test, she didn't grill me about my strange behavior. We wished each other luck and rushed into our classrooms.

I felt better about this test than the last one, even though a little part of me hated to admit it, since the hacker was the one who'd given me this opportunity. I was more familiar with the concepts (Hailey was right!) and I was able to dive right in. After all the tests were handed in, Mrs. Birnbaum sat on the edge on her desk, took off her black glasses, and addressed the class.

"So we've certainly learned something through this process," she said. "I'd love you all to take a look at Samantha Martone and Michael Lawrence's fantastic article covering the story. It really opens up a great discussion about this incident. One you all, I hope, will continue having, so we never find ourselves in this spot again. The Know-It-All letter is also a great one that illustrates the same topic. I think most discussions around these articles will lead to one conclusion: that cheaters always lose."

I wanted to jump up with joy. I didn't, of

course, but I couldn't help beaming. I glanced around and everyone was nodding and calling out things like, "Good job, Sam!" Except for Will Hutchins. As usual, he kept his eyes straight ahead, his face shaded by his hood. I looked at him a little more closely and noticed a small smile on his face. Interesting. I really hoped that what Michael heard was true, that we were actually going to find out what happened!

I floated through the rest of my day. The paper was out—check. Second math test taken—check. Now all I had to do was get through the rest of the day. Then it would be Spring Fling. During my last class of the day—which also happened to have Michael in it—our teacher reached into her desk and pulled out a pile of papers and asked a student to hand them out. "This is being handed out to all students at the same time," she said. "Please read it carefully and share it with your parents." I grabbed mine, my heart in my throat, and my eyes raced over the words.

Dear students and parents,

The recent security breach of the math department's computer files has been traced back to a student at our school. This student has been suspended for three weeks and will begin a mandatory counseling and tutoring program in order to help this person make better academic and ethical decisions in the future. At this time, the school will not be pressing charges. Our systems are now much better protected and should not be vulnerable to any security breaches in the future. Much appreciation goes to the IT consultants who were brought in to resolve the matter, along with all the members of the IT club, led by Will Hutchins, for their assistance in the research and in rebuilding our system. I hope we have learned as a school that no one wins in a situation like this and that we can work together to continue to be honest, upstanding citizens of Cherry Valley Middle School. Please address any further concerns you have about this matter to me.

Sincerely,

Principal Pfeiffer

Michael and I met each other in the hallway, each gripping the notice.

"Are you thinking what I'm thinking?" he said.

"Probably. This means Will didn't do it," I said in a low voice. "He's in the IT club. He was on the good guy team this whole time. Huh. I guess you can't jump to conclusions until you really know the facts."

"Spoken like a true reporter."

"Do you think we'll ever know who it was?" I asked.

"I guess we will, eventually. It can't stay a secret forever. People will figure it out. I don't think anyone I know well was absent today."

"Me neither." I did feel some sympathy for the hacker now that it was all over. He or she was probably pretty scared and confused right now. Hopefully they would get the help they needed. It wasn't going to be an easy road for them.

When we walked out of school together, I saw a few people go up to Will and pat him on the back. His hood was off and he looked happier than I had ever seen him. Once again, I learned that things are never exactly how they appear.

The next day the sun was shining and it was a little warm for spring, perfect amusement park weather. After all that had happened I was ready for a day off. It seemed like everyone was, and we were all smiling and joking. Hailey and I walked around, stuffing our faces with cotton candy and soft pretzels and trying out all the wimpy rides. I wasn't sure if my stomach could handle anything serious after all the junk I had eaten. I was kind of excited about the prospect of the Ferris wheel with Michael. Hailey and I had worked out a plan so we'd all be standing in front of it at the same time.

But then we saw Michael standing in front of the Triple Terror Roller Coaster. He came over to us with a gleam in his eye.

"Hey, Paste, want to go on it with me?" he said, pointing behind his back at the monstrous black and red roller coaster, which sped backward, forward, and went upside down. I had never been on anything close. I shook my head.

"Don't tell me the girl who's not afraid to ask

anyone anything if it's for the paper is scared to go on that?"

I gave Hailey a helpless look. This wasn't the Ferris wheel plan at all.

"You go, girl," Hailey said, a giddy thrill in her voice.

"What about you?" I asked.

"Someone needs to take pictures!" She whipped out her digital camera, running over to a nearby bench. ***Best Friend Abandons Ship!*** Before I knew what was happening, Michael grabbed my arm and led me up the steps toward the line. This was not what I'd imagined. Well, the arm grabbing was. But not the pulsing fear that was running through my body.

I held on to Michael's arm for dear life as we twisted backward, forward, and upside down. I knew I was holding his arm, but I wasn't holding it and getting a nice warm feeling. I was getting a terrified "oh my goodness what have I done please get me off" feeling. When I got off, my head was really spinning and the color had drained from my face.

"You okay?" Michael asked, now truly

concerned. "Let's find you a seat. Gosh. I'm sorry. I didn't want to make you sick."

"I'm fine," I said in a shaky voice. Then he put his arm around me and guided me to a bench. His arm around me made my knees buckle even more and kind of blew the Ferris wheel fantasy out of the water. If only I hadn't felt like I was going to throw up. Michael and Hailey sat with me for a while as I tried to settle myself. Then Hailey decided to go on a few rides with Jenna and Kristen and left me sitting alone with Michael.

After a while Michael asked me if I wanted to get up and walk around for a bit. "You look a little better," he said.

"I'll try." Maybe moving around would make me feel less nauseous. I wasn't going to let anything ruin my Spring Fling. I deserved this! We went over to the game section. There was a game where you had to throw a baseball at a moving catcher's mitt. Michael went right over to it. I followed.

"Watching me play isn't going to make you sick, is it?" Michael asked, still worried.

"Don't be silly. Go play." I pointed to the

game. He went over and let his baseball expertise take over. Every ball he threw landed hard in the catcher's mitt. He missed only the last one. The man running the game handed him a huge pink-and-yellow stuffed elephant. He took it and proudly offered it to me.

"If this doesn't make you feel better, I don't know what will!" he said.

"Awww, but I already have one," I responded.

He looked crestfallen.

"I'm kidding!" I said, taking the elephant.

"If you're making jokes, then you must feel better," he said. He smiled and his bright blue eyes sparkled at me. "Working with you is always a great roller-coaster ride, Pasty!"

"You too, Mikey," I said, trying to sound nonchalant, but inside I was thrilled. I clutched the elephant and noticed that I didn't feel that sick anymore. "I think my new friend cured me." I held up the elephant. Then I gave it a little hug. I wished I could give Michael Lawrence a hug, but I wasn't sure I should. Plus, I still felt a little queasy.

I realized that maybe my plans didn't always go as I expected. You can picture something in your mind right down to the last detail, but that doesn't mean it's going to happen exactly that way. There will always be twists and turns. But sometimes the revised version is even better than the original.

Extra! Extra!

Want the scoop on what Samantha is up to next?

Here's a sneak peek of the seventh book in the Dear Know-It-All series:

Black and White and Gray All Over

FOREIGN STRANGER STEALS GIRL'S LIFE!

I don't want to brag, but I think my dream of becoming a reporter one day is well on its way to really happening. I write a lot of articles for the *Cherry Valley Voice*, my middle school newspaper (okay, not just I—I write with my supercrush, Michael Lawrence). But our last few articles especially have gotten a lot of praise. Kids stop me in the hall and say things like *I really liked what you wrote about Pay to Play* or *Way to go on your coverage of the cheating scandal!* It's totally cool and it feels great!

I also get lots of anonymous compliments because I write the advice column called Dear Know-It-All for the paper. No one at school, and I mean *no one*—not even my best friend, Hailey Jones—knows that I am the Know-It-All this year, but I do overhear kids saying really nice things about the Know-It-All responses (My responses!) in the paper. All this, plus Mr. Trigg, the faculty advisor for the *Voice*, has taken to automatically giving me and Michael the plum assignments. He calls us the Dream Team, his "star reporters." I love it! Of course, I'd love anything officially linking me with Michael, Mr. Cutie himself.

Sadly, my nearest and dearest just don't get it. Like yesterday, I was tutoring Hailey for her grammar exam (she's dyslexic, and I always help her with her studying for tests), and I said something flat out, just a fact, and she got annoyed with me. All I said was, "You're lucky your best friend happens to be the best writer in the school." I'm not making it up. It's a fact. But Hailey told me I need to get over myself. I mean, maybe Michael Lawrence is as good a writer as I am, but it's not like he's going to tutor Hailey, right? I was just making conversation, stating the obvious. I don't know why she got so upset about it.

Then at dinner I was telling my mom and my older sister, Allie, about a new writing camp I'd like to attend this summer and how I have to be nominated by a teacher at school in order to apply. I said it's a total no-brainer because Mr. Trigg will do it for me. After all, besides Michael, there's really no one on the newspaper staff who's as good as I am. It's just a fact. But Allie was all snide and said, "Oh, sorry! I forgot about all those Pulitzer Prizes you've won," and my mom (*my very own mom!*) told me not to get a big head. Whatever, people. I am all about facts, and this is just a fact: I'm a great reporter.

Today we have our staff meeting for the next issue, when Mr. Trigg will dole out the assignments for our new articles, and I can't wait. I know I'll get to work with Michael again (hello, quality time with my crushie!) and I know I'll get a juicy, hard-hitting article to report, and I know Mr. Trigg will sing my praises in public like he always does.

I got to the newsroom a little early in order to get a good seat and save a spot for Michael, who always dashes in at the last minute. I snagged the little sofa just inside the door—the best spot— and I spread out my stuff to keep people away from Michael's half of the sofa. Then I pulled out my latest fresh notebook and began making a list of things I need to do after school today, including stop by the Dear Know-It-All mailbox to collect any new letters and check my bank balance to see if I can afford to buy two new long skirts—kind of my new trademark look—since Allie pointed out that mine are all trashed at the bottom hems. I hate to shop and find it totally boring, plus it kills me to spend money on clothes, but Allie insists on it when the things I own get too dingy.

The newsroom filled up, and sure enough, just as Mr. Trigg came out of his office and strode to the front of the room, Michael popped in the door. He looked at me on the sofa and gestured to the empty spot (as if it wasn't him I was saving it for!). I nodded and quickly cleared my things, and he settled in right next to me, totally cozy. I had to take a moment to think, *This is one of the happiest days of my life.*

I smiled and sighed and turned my attention to Mr. Trigg, who is British and charming and very witty.

"Good morning, gang! Glad to see you all! Righty-ho, we have lots to discuss today . . ." He rifled through a pile of papers in his hand and found the one he was looking for. "Aha! Yes! Hmm. Here!" He looked up and scanned the room. Despite Mr. Trigg's kind of careless appearance—his tall, lanky frame stooped as usual, his suit wrinkled and bagging, and his trademark scarf hanging limply around his neck—he is an exacting journalist and an enthusiastic one. He was as excited today as he always is when starting a new issue, and his excitement was contagious.

"I've got an interesting clipping here on year-round school, something I think we should explore. . . ."

There were groans around the room, but Mr. Trigg shushed everyone with a smile. "It's getting quite popular round the world these days. Hmm. Let's see what this article says. Students receive the same number of vacation days as always. Breaks are more frequent but shorter. . . . Shorter breaks increase knowledge retention. . . . You know, students do tend to forget quite a lot over the summer," he said conversationally. "In addition . . . blah, blah, blah . . . the school buildings don't stand empty . . . easier for working parents . . . and so forth. Quite interesting, I daresay. Now, who should it go to . . . ?"

He looked up and surveyed the room, and his eyes stopped on me and Michael. I'd known we were going to get it from the moment he started telling us about it. It just felt like a me and Michael article—big, juicy, timely, lots of research . . .

But suddenly the door to the newsroom opened and everyone looked up.

"Oh, hello! Pardon me, but is this the newspaper meeting?"

In the doorway was a very pretty girl my age. She had black, wavy hair, a pale, creamy complexion, and bright blue eyes, and she spoke with an English accent, to boot! She was smiling and didn't seem at all nervous to be interrupting.

Mr. Trigg was very welcoming. "Well, hello! This *is* the newspaper meeting. Won't you join us, Ms. . . . ?"

"Bigley! Kate Bigley. I was wondering if you

might need any more writers. I've just arrived, transferred in from—"

"Manchester, England, right?" Mr. Trigg interrupted, pointing his finger at her as a huge smile lit up his face.

Kate Bigley laughed and blushed prettily. "Why, yes! And you . . . Liverpool, right?"

Mr. Trigg guffawed and slapped his leg. "Yes, indeed. Well done! Wonderful to have someone from the mother country in our midst! And we've always got room for more reporters."

Kate Bigley said, "That's awfully kind, Mr. . . . ?"

"Trigg. Mr. Trigg. Welcome aboard. Now, we were just discussing an article we'd like to do on year-round schooling. . . ."

"Oh, we have that back home. It was all over the papers when they started. Quite the controversy at first, but everything seems settled now in the schools where they've got it. My friends are all a bit worried it's coming for everyone!" Kate Bigley perched on the arm of the sofa where Michael and I were sitting and crossed her legs, settling in. All eyes were on her, but she didn't seem to mind one bit. I don't know why this immediately annoyed me, but it did. As did her sitting right next to Michael without even asking if it was okay. This Kate Bigley was pretty forward.

Mr. Trigg's eyes sparkled. "Well, since you have more experience with the topic than the rest of us, why don't you and Mr. Lawrence, who is seated right next to you, take this on for our next issue? He's got lots of experience and can show you the ropes. You're in very good hands, Ms. Bigley."

Michael nodded up at her, and she smiled back, nodding too.

"Wonderful," she said.

Wonderful? How about *horrible?!* I wanted to throw up. I felt a hot blush starting, a mix of both anger and mortification. How could Mr. Trigg just cut me out like that? He knew that was my article! How could this girl sandbag him in just minutes, stealing my crush and my assignment in one fell swoop?

All three of them were smiling in the aftermath of their little lovefest, and I was seething.